What Might Have Been

TULSA

ISBN: 978-1-957262-30-7
What Might Have Been

Yorkshire Publishing
1425 E 41st Pl
Tulsa, OK 74105
www.YorkshirePublishing.com
918.394.2665

Published in the USA

By

Jackie Boos

Chapter One

I couldn't believe my eyes. I had to rub them and readjust just to make sure I wasn't dreaming. Standing before me in a small coffee shop in Austin was the former love of my life.

I had come down to Austin from Fort Worth to escape the rapidly deteriorating wreckage that was my marriage and to get some much-needed "me time."

He caught my eye, and a flicker of recognition crossed his face. He smiled at me with that friendly, easygoing smile of his and proceeded to head toward my table.

His hair had grown longer but was still shiny as ever and he wore it in a ponytail. He still had that knowing twinkle in his eye as if he was both well-aware of, and yet oblivious to, the kind of attention his looks garnered from every woman in every room he walked into.

"Hey, Shelby," he said casually as he reached my table.

"Well, hello Aiden," I replied. "What brings you to Austin?"

"I'm working on some finishing touches to my new album with a producer down here," he said.

Aiden's popularity in music had grown exponentially since our breakup. The man that I had once sat with at a piano to write simple love songs was now a household name. I had followed his career (how could I not?) and kept track of when and where he was going on tour but didn't muster up enough guts to actually attend one of his shows. He had tried to contact me numerous times over the years, but I just couldn't bring myself to reply. That was another life, and I was another person.

For the last 15 years, I had lost sight of who I once was and how I had envisioned my life playing out.

Once upon a time, I was a songwriter who saw myself writing the world's greatest love songs for the world's premier voices to sing. I had terrible stage fright and could never gather enough courage to go up on stage and sing my own songs. That's where Aiden came in.

We had met one night at one of the bars in our little college town. We were both there to hear friends play during open mic night.

We struck up a conversation and discovered we both had a love for Motown music, coffee, and Italian food.

By the end of the night, we had each other's numbers and a date for two nights later. After the first few dates, we discovered how much we had in common and how much we enjoyed each other's company.

Being with Aiden felt so easy and natural. After a few weeks, we professed our love for one another, and I was soon mentally preparing to take his last name and picking out China patterns.

After several months of falling head-over-heels in love with him, it suddenly all came to a screeching halt.

Chapter Two

Aiden had been writing songs since he was a kid just as I had, but unlike me, he knew how to play several instruments very well and was confident enough to get up on the stage and pour his heart out to an audience. The audience always responded well to his soulful, raspy voice, and the girls in the audience went nuts for his piercing blue eyes.

Lucky for me, I was the one who got to leave with him.

Aiden was able to get gigs every weekend and never had problems filling whatever venue he was in. On one fateful Saturday night, he was playing at Chance's bar to a packed house. It just happened that one of those people filling the seats was a music producer visiting from Nashville.

The producer was shocked to find such a fabulous talent in a small college town. He gave Aiden his contact information, and days later it was a done deal. Aiden broke the news to me after his gig the next Friday night.

"What do you mean you are moving to Nashville? What about the rest of college?" I asked.

"Shelby, this is a once-in-a-lifetime opportunity. I can always go back to college and finish my degree, but how often does a record producer offer to help me get my songs recorded?" he replied.

"What about all of those songs we were writing together?" I asked.

"You can come with me, and we'll record them together," he said.

"I can't just pack up and move to Nashville. I'll lose my scholarship, and you know I can't perform on stage. Am I just supposed to follow you around like a groupie with no career or degree to fall back on?" I was near tears at this point.

"Couldn't you just take a semester off and see what happens? I really don't want to lose you," he was starting to get teared up himself.

"Aiden, we've only been together for a few months. I really can't make that kind of commitment to you right now. It's not as if we're getting married or anything…"

"Then let's get married! You can come on the road with me, and then we can have a whole slew of kids and take them on the road with us, too. You're basically a teacher already. You can just teach all of them on the tour bus. Plus, we can still write songs together and record them. Think of how much fun it would be to travel together and have our little family on the road!"

"Aiden, really think about what you are asking of me. I can't just uproot my life and take off on a tour bus with you. I want to finish my degree, plus my family is all here. What would all of them think if I just took off for Nashville with a guy I met only a few months ago? It's just not practical."

"I know it's not practical, but it's what my heart wants. I don't want to sacrifice my dreams, and I don't want to sacrifice our relationship. Why can't I just have both?" He was visibly in tears at this point, as was I.

"Please don't make me choose," he begged.

"Aiden, I'm sorry, but I just can't go with you. I understand that you must follow your dream. Maybe we can figure out a way to do the long-distance relationship thing." As soon as the words came out of my mouth, I knew that would never happen. Of course, these kinds of things never worked out.

We went back to his apartment that night and made love for what we knew would be the last time. It was slow, passionate, and soft. It was as if our bodies were saying the words our lips could never speak.

The next morning, I helped him pack his things and load them into the moving truck. With each box we lifted, my heart felt heavier and heavier.

When the last box was finally loaded, we knew the time had come to say the words we didn't want to say.

Aiden looked at me knowingly and drew me in for a hug. Then he pulled away and gave me a slow, soft kiss. I didn't want to come up for air.

"I don't think I can bring myself to say goodbye," he said.

"Then don't. Just call me when you get there, and we'll take it from there," I said.

He got in the truck and started driving away. I held it together until I got back to my apartment. The second I closed the door, the floodgates opened, and I collapsed on the floor in tears.

After an hour, I peeled myself off the floor and dragged myself into bed where I willed myself to sleep. I had been sleeping for seven hours when my phone woke me at 9:00 p.m. It was Aiden.

I took one look at my phone, muted it, and fell back asleep until morning.

Chapter Three

I was sitting in the coffee house contemplating what to say next to Aiden. Were we just going to make small talk with each other like we were just running into a classmate from high school?

"How long are you in town for?" I ventured.

"Probably about a week or so," he replied. "Mind if I join you?"

"Oh, my goodness. Where are my manners? Of course, you can join me," I said.

Aiden sat down next to me, and it was as if no time had passed. We began discussing our current life, what we had been up to since college, basically filling in the gaps since we had last seen each other. Before I knew it, two hours had evaporated.

Aiden checked his phone and seemed to just realize how late it was getting.

"Oh, geez. I've really got to go," he said. Then, after a moment's hesitation, he added, "Do you want to maybe stop by the studio and hear what I've been working on? I mean unless you're busy."

I thought about his offer for a moment. I had only planned on grabbing a coffee and then going shopping. This was supposed to be a "mental health" weekend for myself away from my family to really reconnect to the person I used to be.

Maybe Aiden was the catalyst I needed to find that woman again.

"Sure. I'd love to have a listen," I told him.

His face lit up as he grinned from ear to ear. "That's great! Are you busy now, or do you want to come with me right now?"

"I can come now, that's no problem," I replied. Secretly, I wanted to check in to my hotel room, put on a sexier outfit, and reapply my makeup first, but I was not about to let on that he still had that kind of effect on me.

"Great. I only have my motorcycle right now, so I hope you don't mind," he said.

"So, you're a motorcycle guy now, huh?"

"Well, I used to ride dirt bikes a while back, but being a musician, the motorcycle becomes more appealing to gain street cred." He smiled. This guy that poured his heart out through ballads and tender love songs was looking to gain street cred.

I had never ridden a motorcycle before, so I really wasn't sure what to expect. I hopped on the back, put on the helmet, and placed my arms around his waist. As he revved the engine and the bike lurched forward, I tightened my grip, grabbing him in a bear hug for fear of falling off. I couldn't tell if that was an accidental move or not, but I was immediately drawn to the scent of leather and espresso that rose from his warm body.

As we sped through the streets of Austin, I began daydreaming about what life would have been like if I had gone with Aiden to Nashville. Would I have been able to live on a tour bus with him and raise kids? What about the times I couldn't go with him? Would I be able to endure months without seeing my husband and essentially raising the kids on my own?

In college, it didn't seem like something I could handle. I wanted a husband with a 9-to-5 job, values similar to mine. I had wanted to live in the suburbs and raise our family while I taught school and spent time with the kids during the summer.

That is exactly what I had, and look where that had gotten me. I don't even recognize myself anymore. I am just Dave's wife and Billy and Bonnie's mom. There was no "me" anymore. I was just the person who was there to do everyone else's bidding. I couldn't even remember the last time I had written a song or picked up a guitar.

By the time we got to the studio, I quickly forced myself to snap out of my reverie. What the hell was I doing? I knew I still had unresolved feelings for Aiden, and here I was spending more time with him, even though I was a married woman. I was venturing into dangerous territory.

As we walked into the studio, Aiden introduced me to the producer and the engineer he was working with on the album.

"Aiden, I think the latest ballad needs a little tweaking on the vocals," said the producer, Jim.

"Sure, Jim. I'll get in there and see what I can do," Aiden replied.

I took a seat on the leather studio couch and watched as Aiden put on the headphones and stepped up to the mic. I tried to imagine what it must be like to do this for a living. What if we had actually recorded one of the songs we had written together? The thought of hearing my own lyrics being sung on a record thrilled me.

Aiden began with that sexy, breathy voice he reserved for ballads.

"Looking back, it's hard to see
What went wrong between you and me
All I know is I regret
Not holding on from the time we met

I should have held you tight and never let you go

Things are so different now

From how I thought our life would go
Can we just turn back time
And this time I won't let you go

Then I won't have to ask myself every day
What I could do differently this time to make you stay
What could I have done way back then
So, I don't constantly think about
What might have been."

I could feel the tears streaming down my face as I ran out the door of the studio.

Was I just imagining it, or was he really considering how his life would have been different with me in it?

I didn't wait around to ask. I hailed a cab and told the driver to head to the hotel as quickly as possible.

Chapter Four

After about two hours of not wanting to leave my hotel room, I heard a knock at the door. I opened it to find Aiden on the other side.

"What happened back there?" he asked me.

"How did you find me?" I retorted.

"I bribed the taxi driver who drove you here and then asked the front desk which room was yours. The girl up front is a fan," he said.

"I'm sorry, Aiden. I guess I just wasn't ready to face you and what we used to have," I replied.

"I'm sorry if I scared you off in any way. I just wanted you to hear my new stuff and tell me what you think. I value your opinion since you are such a talented songwriter," he said.

"That song you just sang really struck a nerve with me," I nervously responded.

"*What Might Have Been?* Why do you say that?" he asked.

"Well, isn't it about me?" I couldn't even stand to look him in the eye while I asked.

"Why would you assume it is about you?" he smiled. "You think pretty highly of yourself, don't you?"

I was mortified. I must have turned about five shades of red. "It wasn't about me? Wow. I feel really stupid," I replied.

"Don't feel bad. I can see how you would think that. It's been 17 years since we've been together, Shelby. I hate to break it to you, but I have dated other girls since then." His easy smile was reassuring. "Why don't we start over again. Do you have any plans for dinner tonight?"

"Yes, that would be nice," I relaxed a little. "I'm really sorry about the way I behaved earlier. I don't know what got into me."

"You have to stop running away from me all the time," Aiden said. "Am I really that scary?"

"No, of course not," I smiled at him. The truth was I was a little scared. Just seeing Aiden was bringing back all of those old feelings. I couldn't allow myself to feel that way again. I was a married woman with two children. I didn't want to get myself into a sticky situation.

Later that night, we met at a hip downtown Austin restaurant. Aiden had specifically asked for a table away from the rest of the crowd so as not toattract attention. It felt so strange to try to avoid being seen by people. I felt like a spy.

As the night went on, we reminisced about the past and then moved on to the touchy subject of our current relationships.

"So, you have been married for 15 years and have two children?" he asked.

"Yes, Billy and Bonnie. They're named after Billy Joel and Bonnie Raitt," I said.

"How cute is that?" he replied. "What is your husband's name?"

"Dave. We met not long after you and I stopped seeing each other," just thinking about that moment caused pain in my chest. "I'm sorry about the way things ended, by the way."

"Don't worry about it. That was ages ago. The whole long-distance thing probably wouldn't have worked for me back then anyway."

"So, how are things working for you now? Are you married?"

"Yes, I am. I have been for about 12 years. No kids yet, but we've been trying. They'll come when they are supposed to."

"I see. How did you two meet?"

"I actually met her after one of my concerts," he replied. "She was friends with one of my band members, and we got to talking afterward and really hit it off. She's really great."

I really didn't want to sit there and listen to how great his wife was and how wonderful her life was with him in it. I didn't want to think about the fact that I was so close to having that as my own life. I quickly changed the subject.

"So, when does the new album come out?" I asked him.

"It's supposed to be released in three months. There are a lot of obstacles in the way right now, but that's the plan. We are going to do a European tour first and then the U.S. tour, which is a little unconventional. I haven't been to Europe in a few years, though."

"That sounds wonderful," I said. "I've always wanted to go to Europe."

"Have you been doing any songwriting lately?" he asked.

"Just a little bit here and there. I've been so busy with my job and the kids that I haven't really had much time. Plus, you know that I must really be inspired to start writing. Not much inspiration has struck lately."

"I know what you mean. Sometimes it's like pulling teeth to get a song out of me. I've been working with a lot of other writers lately. We collaborate together, but there haven't been many songs I've written on my own in a while," he thought a minute. "Would you maybe want to work on something together? You know, see if we've still got it?"

I thought hard for a moment. "Actually, I think that would be great. Maybe it's the kick I need to really get back to songwriting."

We decided to meet the next morning at his hotel. He had a suite booked at one of the swanky downtown Austin hotels. I couldn't believe how large it was. I had never been in a room so nice before. He had a grand piano in his hotel room. We both sat down and got to work.

"So, you say you haven't had any inspiration lately, huh? Maybe we can just be each other's muses," Aiden said.

"Maybe. We used to crank out songs fairly quickly," I said.

"That's true. I have this little chord progression I've been working on. Why don't you give it a listen?" he asked.

Aiden played some of a melody he had been working on. It was an upbeat, folksy-type tune. Something I could definitely see fitting in with his typical songs.

"That sounds great!" I said. "It sounds like one of those melodies that is meant to tell the story of some legend and how he came to be."

"That is a great idea! I haven't done a song like that in ages!" Aiden looked elated. "Let's start brainstorming some ideas about this legend."

We sat at the piano for a while, playing around with different sounds and lyrics, and after a while moved to the acoustic guitar. It felt so good to get back to music. I couldn't remember the last time I had tried to write a song. When I was with Aiden, everything seemed to come so naturally. It didn't feel like work at all. It just felt like fun. I was starting to let my guard down and really feel like myself.

After about three hours of songwriting, Aiden said he had a meeting to get to.

"This was really great," he said. "I can't believe how well we work together. I had forgotten how well we gel. I feel like you're the master lyricist, and I am just the soundtrack to your beautiful words."

I blushed. "I don't know about "master lyricist." I feel really rusty trying to crank out these lyrics. It does feel good to get back into it, though."

We sat and stared at each other for what felt like hours, but was probably more like 10 seconds. I fought the strong urge to lean in for a kiss. Aiden looked like he was contemplating the exact same thing.

"Well, I better get going," he said. "How long are you in town for?"

"I'm leaving tomorrow morning," I answered.

"I hope we can see each other before you take off. It's been great spending time with you these past couple of days," he said.

"Yes, it has," I replied. "I'll give you a call, and we can maybe meet one last time for a coffee before I head home."

"That sounds wonderful," he replied. "And Shelby?"

"Yeah?"

"Don't ever put music on the back burner. You are a natural songwriter and shouldn't give it up. You have it in your blood. Please don't stop making music." "I suppose you're right. Life just gets in the way sometimes, though, you know?"

"What do you mean? Doesn't your husband support you writing songs?"

"Not exactly. It doesn't exactly bring home the bacon," I replied. "I have two kids to feed, so I need to focus on that."

"Just please don't lose sight of who you are. At one point in time, I fell in love with that woman. I don't want to see her disappear." With that, he walked out the door to his meeting.

Chapter Five

All night, I tossed and turned in bed thinking about what Aiden had said to me. I had felt that I was losing sight of who I was for a very long time, but to hear someone else say it made it even more of a reality.

As I was getting ready to meet Aiden for coffee in the morning, I started thinking about what exactly I was going to say to Dave when I returned home. Things had gotten so bad between us that I wasn't even sure why we were trying to make it work. We didn't feel like a married couple anymore. We just felt like strangers living in the same house. He was working twelve-hour days at the office and was so stressed out that as soon as he got home, all he wanted to do was sit on the couch in front of the TV with a beer in hand. It was all up to me to keep up with the kids' activities, prepare meals, keep the house clean, while working a 50-hour a week job on top of everything else. I felt like Dave only saw me as a housekeeper and cook. There was no romance, no loving looks, no deep meaningful conversations. By the time we put the kids to bed every night, we were both so exhausted that we immediately fell asleep ourselves. We still made love occasionally, but it was always on his terms, which meant that I was never in the mood and hadn't had an orgasm in years.

I arrived at the coffee shop to find Aiden sitting alone, sipping an espresso. He was wearing my favorite shirt of his and a leather jacket. The blue of the shirt brought out the blue in his eyes. He was staring out the window and seemed deep in thought. He looked up, almost surprised to see me.

"Shelby, hey," he said.

"Hi, Aiden. This is a great little coffee shop," I replied.

"Yeah, it's one of my favorites here in Austin. Most people flock to Starbucks, but I prefer this place. They always have great specials," he answered. "Listen, Shelby. I've been doing a lot of thinking, and I have a proposition for you."

"What is it?" I asked, afraid of what he was going to say next.

"I am going to L.A. in a few weeks to mix this album, and I want you to join me out there. I was thinking we could maybe even record some of your songs," he said.

"I don't know, Aiden. I have a lot of stuff going on at home. I don't know if I can just leave the kids behind," I said.

"It won't be that long," he said. "Just a few days. We could record some of the stuff we've written together. Wouldn't it be great to have some of your songs recorded instead of just sitting in a notebook somewhere?"

The mention of recording my songs both excited me and struck fear inside of me. I had always wanted to record my songs, but I was also afraid for people to hear some of them. Some of the songs I had written really bared my soul. There were even a couple I had written about Aiden since our breakup, and I wasn't sure I was ready for him to hear them.

"That does sound tempting. I'll think about it," I answered him.

"Well, don't think about it for too long. The clock is ticking. I'll need an answer in the next week or so," he said.

We sat there a little while longer, discussing different musicians we had been listening to lately and how their work inspired us. We talked about different song ideas, and Aiden talked about where he would be going on his European tour and how much he was looking forward to it. Before I knew it, it was time to leave.

"Aiden, it was so nice seeing you and catching up," I said.

"You as well. It's so strange that we just happened to bump into each other here. I really like the songs we worked on. I hope you seriously consider coming out to L.A. with me. Natasha is coming with me, so you would get to meet her as well," he said.

The mention of his wife's name struck a chord with me. I had nothing against her, but for some reason, I didn't even want to hear her name. The thought of him being happy with another woman was still not appealing to me.

"I will think about it," I said. "Goodbye, Aiden. Good luck with the new album and everything."

"Thanks, Shelby. I guess I'll see you around," he said.

I looked back at him one more time before heading out the door. Thinking back to seeing him drive away in that moving truck, I was sure that was the last time I would ever see him. Seeing him again stirred up so many oldmemories and emotions, I wasn't quite sure what to make of them. I knew that I had a husband and children waiting for me back at home, but something inside me had changed that weekend. Aiden brought out a part of me that I thought was long gone. Maybe it was time the old me resurfaced.

Chapter Six

As soon as I arrived back home, Billy and Bonnie rushed to greet me with warm hugs. It felt so good to see their smiling faces, and it ended up being a bit of a reality check for me. It felt like I had been living in a fantasy land for the last few days, and now I was back where I belonged. Dave didn't seem to share the children's excitement in my return.

"Did you enjoy your little trip?" he asked with a sarcastic tone to his voice.

"It was nice to get away for a little bit and reconnect with myself," I told him, ignoring the fact that he wasn't being the least bit sincere with me.

"Well, I hope you liked it and got it out of your system because that's never happening again," Dave said.

"What is that supposed to mean?" I asked him.

"I don't have time to take care of the kids every time you have a mental breakdown and decide to leave," he said.

"Dave, I did not have a mental breakdown, and they are your kids too. Why is the responsibility solely on me?" I asked.

I could see the anger start to show itself on his face and could feel it brewing inside of me as well. I didn't want to start fighting in front of the kids, so I quickly changed gears.

"Why don't we just discuss this in private later. I would rather not have this conversation in front of the kids," I said. I turned to Billy. "What did you guys do while I was gone?"

"We watched some movies upstairs while Daddy watched football downstairs and drank beers," he replied.

I tried to hide my disappointment with Dave. "That sounds like a lot of fun. Did you watch anything new and exciting?"

"No. We just watched some of our old movies. Daddy didn't want to take us to rent anything new," Bonnie said.

I couldn't help but think that this was a huge, wasted opportunity for Dave to reconnect with the kids. He barely got to see them these days because he was so busy with work. Why wouldn't he want to take this chance to spend more time with them?

"I brought you guys some souvenirs," I told the kids.

"How much money did you send when you were down there?" asked Dave. "Was I just stuck at home so you could go out and spend all of my money?"

"Dave, I really don't want to get into all of this in front of the kids," I said, trying to hide the fury bubbling up inside of me. "Billy, Bonnie, why don't you two take your new toys to your rooms and play with them while Mommy and Daddy catch up for a little bit? Then I'll cook some dinner and we'll sit down as a family and talk about our weekend."

The kids walked off to their rooms, and I gave Dave a look that I hope conveyed how extremely disappointed I was to have to come home to this kind of confrontation. All the calmness, peace, and happiness I felt over the weekend had immediately disappeared. Now all I felt was sadness, anger, and defeat.

"Listen, Dave," I said. "I know things haven't been that great between us lately, but there is no need to tear into me in front of the kids."

"I will tell you whatever I feel like telling you, whenever I feel like telling you. You are not the boss of me," he replied.

"I realize that, but I wish you would realize that the kids are soaking up every word you say to me, and when you put down their mother right in front of them, they aren't going to have much respect for her. They learn from your example," I said.

"Don't try to psychoanalyze me and my behavior!" Dave exploded. "I've heard enough from you about how I am doing everything wrong and am a terrible father! I work so incredibly hard to put food on the table for this family, and I don't need my wife telling me how I'm doing everything wrong. Why can't you just be a supportive wife and take care of the kids and the cooking while I take care of doing the work?"

"You do realize that I work too, don't you?" I replied. "How is it fair for you to ask me to take on sole responsibility for the kids and the house in addition to working a full-time job? Marriage is supposed to be a partnership, and our kids need a father, not a corporate sponsor!"

I felt totally defeated. We had been going round and round for years on these very same topics, and nothing was getting resolved and nothing was changing. I was so tired of dealing with the constant battles, and I was exhausted with balancing my job, the kids, the house, and trying to keep Dave happy on top of everything else. I wanted a chance at happiness as well.

Over the past few years, my feelings of depression had grown to the point where I began constantly contemplating suicide as an escape from this feeling of being trapped and in pain 24/7. If it wasn't for the kids, I probably would have been gone long ago. The constant put-downs, yelling, and feelings of inferiority were getting worse and worse, and I knew I just couldn't take it anymore. It seemed we were at a turning point, and I needed to decide whether to keep living with the pain or to take a stand for myself and my children.

I took a deep breath before addressing the elephant in the room. "Dave, I've been thinking about this for a very long time, and I really think we should get a divorce."

"A divorce?! Do you think you are going to find some other guy you can manipulate to take care of you? You think you can find some other guy to just push around into doing whatever you want him to do?!" Dave spoke with ill suppressed fury apparent in his voice.

"I can't deal with the constant criticism and feelings of failure anymore," I replied in a calm tone. "I try so hard every day, but I'm starting to lose sight of who I once was. I have been slowly losing my will to live."

"You have such a great life that I've provided for you. How could you possibly not appreciate everything I do for you? I have always given you everything you've needed, and I never once laid a hand on you," Dave said.

"I know you have never physically abused me," I replied. "But you must realize that there are other kinds of abuse too. Sometimes I just wish that you would physically hurt me so I would at least have something to show for it." I couldn't stop the tears from flowing at this point. "I am hurt so deep down, and I don't even think you realize how badly you have hurt me or even when you are hurting me. The words that you say to me cut me through like a knife. I feel like a shell of a human being when I'm with you. I just go through the motions without really giving thought to myself or what I might think about what I am doing or how we are living our life. I am tired of living that way, and I want my life back. That is why I needed this weekend to myself. So that I could re-examine my life and decide what I really wanted."

"And you came to the conclusion that you are tired of living a comfortable life with a devoted husband and children?" Dave asked accusingly.

"It's not about our house or how much money we have. I would live in a box if it meant that I could be happy," I told him. "I don't even know who this person is that I have turned into, but it sure isn't me. I'm going to take the kids and go stay with my mom for a few days. I'll come back to get the rest of the stuff later."

"You can't just take the kids! Those are my kids, and I get a say about them!" Dave yelled.

"I'm not taking them away for good. You can still see them. I just thought it would be easier if I still handled the day-to-day things with them," I reasoned with him. "It seemed like you weren't too happy about dealing with them this weekend. Do you really want to be the one always in charge of dealing with them?"

"I don't want you leaving the house at all! You're my wife, and I should get a say in whether or not you leave!" Dave was still yelling.

"Dave, you don't get a say in what I am doing! I may be your wife, but I'm not your slave! I'm an adult and should get a say in how I live my life!" I was heated and screaming at this point. "For our entire marriage, I've dealt with you ordering me around, and I've gone along with it, just trying to be a good wife and mother and not rock the boat. Well, not anymore! I am a human being, too, and I am an adult with a say in how I live my life and what I do in my relationship! I am packing my stuff, and there is nothing you can do about it! If you really want to fight for the kids, you can call the cops or take it up with the judge for all I care, but we are getting out of here tonight!"

I stormed out of the room and couldn't even stand to look at his face anymore. I was so tired of dealing with the emotional abuse that I didn't want to deal with him for one more second. I packed my bag as quickly as I could, got the kids packed up with a week's worth of clothes, and stormed out of the house without one more word to Dave.

Chapter Seven

I stayed at my mom's house for a few days before I filed for a legal separation. Everything felt so unreal to me. I couldn't believe that my marriage was falling apart, and I was seriously considering taking a year off from teaching. I felt like my life couldn't go back to the way it was. Now that I had a taste of songwriting again, I didn't want it to end. One day, out of the blue, I received a phone call from Aiden.

"Last chance to come to Los Angeles with me," he said.

"What?" I replied. I had completely forgotten about Aiden's invitation to work in the studio in Los Angeles.

"We're heading to L.A. next week, so I need an answer right away," he said.

"Aiden, I completely forgot about that. I'm kind of going through a lot of personal things right now, so I'm not sure if I can just pack everything up and head to L.A.," I said.

"Shelby, after writing songs with you in Austin, I haven't stopped thinking about how well we work together. I really think that we can create something great," he said.

I looked at Billy and Bonnie considering if I would be able to spend that time away from them.

"It would only be for three days, Shelby. I'm not asking you to move there or anything," Aiden said.

"Well...I suppose if it's only for a few days, I could probably make it work," I replied.

"Fantastic!" Aiden said. "I'll let the studio guys know and get you a room booked in the same hotel. This is going to be great, Shelby, you'll see."

"I hope you're right. I could use something positive in my life right now," I told him.

A few days later, I packed my bags and said goodbye to my kids. They couldn't quite comprehend why I was leaving and why I wasn't going to be teaching at their school that year. They probably thought I was having some sort of mid-life crisis.

"Don't worry, guys. I'll be back before you know it," I reassured them. "I'll give you a call every night I'm gone to check-in. I'll only be gone for three days. Be good for your grandma, okay?"

"We will, Mom," said Billy.

"Are you sure you want to do this?" my mom asked. "This seems risky. Do you really know this guy anymore? I'm just not sure if it is safe for you."

"I can take care of myself, Mom, but thanks for worrying about me," I replied. "Besides, he's bringing his wife along. It's not like it's just going to be me and him."

"Okay. Just be careful when you're over there. I'll have everything covered here, so don't worry about the kids," she said.

"Thanks again for doing this, Mom. I know it's hard to understand right now, but I feel like it's something I need to do for myself," I told her. I felt like I was telling that to myself even more than I was telling it to her. I needed to constantly reassure myself that I was doing the right thing. I had tried to get Dave involved in taking care of the kids while I was gone, but he said he was much too busy and had no interest in spending extra time with them.

As my plane landed at LAX, a feeling of uneasiness began to well up inside of me. Was I really doing the right thing? Could I even still write songs? What if everything I wrote was total crap? I willed to get a grip and start thinking more positively. This was something I had always wanted to do with my life, and now I was finally doing it. My life hadn't gone on the trajectory I once thought it would, but there is always time to make a change. You are never too old to accomplish your dreams, right?

I checked in to my hotel and told Aiden that I would meet him in the hotel lobby bar for drinks and to meet his wife. I was having mixed feelings about meeting her, but I was glad I would have the alcohol there as a crutch. As I approached the bar, Aiden stood up to greet me looking better than ever. He was wearing his classic tight, black pants and white t-shirt look. The woman who stood up next to him was stunning. She was much shorter than me, but with long, brown wavy hair and large, brown eyes. Her big smile filled up most of her face and came across as friendly and kind.

"Shelby, this is Natasha," Aiden said. "Natasha, this is Shelby. Shelby is going to be working on some songs with me this week. We met back in college and just ran into each other when I was down in Austin."

"It's nice to meet you, Shelby," Natasha said in a southern drawl.

We sat down for drinks, and Natasha recounted the story of how she and Aiden met in Nashville. She gave me basically the same story that Aiden had about them meeting backstage at a concert. They had been married for ten years but hadn't been able to have any children. Aiden's dream of raising kids on the tour bus had ended up being only Natasha and him, exploring the country and the world together. They seemed happy, though.

After a few hours, fatigue from traveling started to take it's toll, and I told them I needed to head up to bed. Aiden said that he would walk me to the elevators.

"So, I have us set up for some studio time tomorrow morning at 9:00 a.m.," he said.

"Sounds great," I replied. "Is there anything I need to bring with me? I have my acoustic and some blank pages for writing."

"That's all you need. I'll have everything else provided for you," he said. "Shelby, I'm really excited we're doing this."

"Me too," I said. "I wasn't so sure at first, but this feels like what I should be doing with my life right now. Everything's been so crazy, but this kind of feels like I'm

coming back to the person I'm meant to be."

"I'm glad to hear it," Aiden said. "I happened to like the person you used to be." He smiled at me. We told each other good night, and then I headed up to my room.

As I got ready for bed, I realized that I felt like I could sleep peacefully for the first time in a long time. I don't know what it was about being around Aiden that comforted me, but I was happy I would get to spend the next few days with him. Even though we weren't in a romantic relationship anymore, there was still something about him that drew me to him and made me feel at peace. As I snuggled into the luxuriously soft hotel bedding, I knew that I could stop focusing on the pain of the past. I could now look ahead to something exciting in my future.

Chapter Eight

The next morning, I woke up feeling refreshed in my super comfortable hotel bed and headed downstairs for some much-needed coffee and breakfast. Although I was incredibly nervous for the day, there was also excitement about what lay ahead. I met Aiden down at the recording studio and found that he had already been working on some things before I even arrived.

"Good morning!" I called walking in.

"Good morning, Shelby!" Aiden said. "Let me introduce you to the producers and engineer. This is Pete, Ed, and Simon. Guys, this is Shelby. You guys are just going to love what she's bringing to the table."

I blushed at Aiden's praise and hoped that I could live up to these kinds of expectations. After introductions and handshakes, we went immediately to work. Aiden and I discussed some songs we had written in the past, and I told him about a few songs I had written by myself over the years. We decided to record some rough vocals and melodies on a few and see how they sounded.

The whole thing was completely out of my comfort zone, and yet somehow, I had never felt more comfortable. Part of me thought about why I hadn't pursued this earlier in my life. It felt so right, like what I was meant to do, so why was I so scared to put it all out there? Songwriting is an incredibly vulnerable thing, and I think I was afraid of how I might come off if I truly put all my feelings out there. Some things are just easier said through song than through an actual conversation. My feelings about Aiden over the years were deeply entrenched into my songs rather than talked about with any other human beings. I had never discussed the breakup with any of my friends or family. Songwriting was my therapy and the only way I felt I could come to terms with my unresolved feelings. I hadn't played any of the songs I wrote about Aiden for him yet, and I was very nervous to get them out in the open. I felt he would read right through me and know exactly what I meant in the lyrics. I decided to share the one I wrote immediately after he left first.

"All I can think about
Is you holding me near.
Whenever you are gone
I wish that you were here.

Why are you so far away?
I wish that you could stay.

Whenever you're gone my world is gray.
I don't think I'll last another day.
Why can't you be here with me?
I'll wish and I'll pray 'till I see you again.

Your voice and your eyes
Staring into my soul,
You better come soon
Before I lose control.

All I can see is you
So, what am I supposed to do?

Whenever you're gone my world is gray.
I don't think I'll last another day.
Why can't you be here with me?
I'll wish and I'll pray 'till I see you again.

Will you come soon so my heart can beat again?
I count the seconds just to see how long it's been.
What can I do?
When can I see you?

Whenever you're gone my world is gray.
I don't think I'll last another day.
Why can't you be here with me?
I'll wish and I'll pray 'till I see you again,
'Till I see you again,
'Till I see you...again.

After our rough recording, I could barely look Aiden in the eye. I wasn't comfortable singing in front of all these strange men, but I also knew that Aiden would know exactly what I meant by the lyrics of that song. The only thing I didn't know for sure was whether he would think I still felt that way, or if he thought it was all in the past. I wasn't even sure I knew the answer to that question.

Hesitantly, I left the recording booth and headed in Aiden's direction. He had an odd look in his eyes that I couldn't quite decipher. It was as if he didn't really know what to make of the song.

"That was great!" said Pete. "That would be a great ballad to include on your record."

"My record?" I asked. "Who said anything about making a record?"

"Oh, I thought Aiden had mentioned to you that we were turning this into a demo," Pete answered, looking confused.

"Aiden, I thought we were just trying some things out. I didn't think we were actually making a demo," I said. "You know how I feel about singing in front of people. I don't want to be the voice on the record. I just want to get my songs out to people who can really sing."

"Shelby, you really need to listen back to this recording," Aiden replied. "I know you don't consider yourself a singer, but I do. You just need to build up your confidence. You're an amazing singer, and I think you would be doing yourself a disservice by not putting out your own songs. Another singer wouldn't have the same emotions behind the song, because she wouldn't be the person who felt those emotions. You have such an earnest way of singing, and everyone can tell that you are really putting your heart out there when you sing your songs rather than just singing someone else's words." He grabbed my hands. "I know it's hard, Shelby. I had a hard time when I first started recording my own songs. It definitely takes some getting used to when you are baring your soul to the world. Oh, but believe me, it's so liberating when you finally decide to let go and just do it."

"I don't know, Aiden, I'm not like you," I told him. "You're just so sure of yourself, and everyone can see how confident you are when you're on stage. I just doubt myself so much, and I think if I perform in front of people they'll see my doubt. Not to mention that I'm singing about my innermost emotions and feelings." I gave him an unsure look.

"But didn't it feel fantastic singing that song you just sang?" Aiden asked.

I contemplated his question. It really did feel pretty good to get everything out in the open. I felt like a big boulder had been lifted off of my chest. I wasn't really scared of other people hearing my song and didn't really care what they thought about my singing ability. If they like it, they'll listen to it. If not, they won't. Simple as that. I wasn't really concerned with having a huge fan following or making a lot of money. I just enjoyed making music. If I was able to continue with this, I could see it being a long-term career.

"It did feel pretty good," I admitted. Then, an idea came to me. Maybe getting everything out in the open would be a new type of therapy for me. I was nervous about Aiden hearing that last song, but there was another one that I wanted to play for him that was just for myself. "Actually, I have a new song that I just wrote a week ago. Maybe you can give me some insight and let me know what you think."

"Fantastic! I'd love to hear it!" Aiden said.

I went back into the recording booth and settled myself in for a song I knew would be gut-wrenching to get out there, but I felt like I needed to.

"What will it take to make me feel like myself again?
What can I do to escape this hibernation den?
I want so bad to be the me I used to be.
Instead of stuck I want to be free.

Is it you, or is it me?
I'm so far from the girl I used to be

Do I have to say goodbye?
Or is there another way?
Do I need to know the why?
Of this pain that won't go away?
I've felt trapped for far too long
And just want to be me.

Is it time I moved from "we" to "me"?

I've been holding back so much
It's killing me inside.
Did I know I agreed to lose myself
When I became your bride?

Is it you, or is it me?
Should I really stay, or is it time I leave?
Do I have to say goodbye,
Or is there another way?
Do I need to know the why
Of this pain that won't go away?
I've felt trapped for far too long
And just want to be me.
Is it time I moved from "we" to "me"?

It hurts to think that we may not be together.
But maybe there's no such thing as forever.
It's buried much too deep.
Not all loves are meant to keep.
Can I just go back to being me?

Do I have to say goodbye?
Or is there another way?
Do I need to know the why
Of this pain that won't go away?
I've felt trapped for far too long,
And just want to be me.
Is it time I moved from "we" to "me"?

Chapter Nine

After I finished singing the song, Aiden took me aside to talk.

"When did you write that song?" he asked.

"Just a week ago," I answered.

"So, can I ask, does this have a personal meaning for you?" Aiden asked.

I let out a huge sigh. "Yes, it does," I admitted.

"Shelby, I'm so sorry," he said as he hugged me. I knew that he would be able to see right through me and know exactly what I was experiencing through my songwriting. "You know what? I think maybe we should be done with recording for today. What do you say to a night on the town tonight with Natasha and me?"

The mention of Natasha's name made me flinch inexplicably. "I don't know if I'm ready for that, Aiden," I said.

"C'mon. It seems to me like you need a night of fun to blow off some steam and take your mind off things," he said.

"Oh, okay," I gave in. I couldn't remember the last time I had been out for a "night on the town." I wasn't even sure what to wear or how to behave. Come to think of it, I hadn't even packed any appropriate attire for something like that. I had just expected to either be in the studio, restaurants, or in my hotel room. I was definitely out of practice when it came to hitting the town. I mentioned my concerns to Aiden.

"Don't worry. We have some time this afternoon. Natasha can take you shopping, and you can find the perfect outfit to wear. It's on me," Aiden said. "We're not going to hit any hip clubs or anything. Let's be honest, we are not 21 anymore. We'll just go to some fun bars and hang out. It will be fantastic! I could use some time to blow off some steam from my hectic schedule as well."

Later that afternoon, I met up with Aiden and Natasha to do a little shopping on Rodeo Drive. I had never been more intimidated in my entire life. Everywhere I looked, there were women who were probably in their fifties, although they looked like they were in their twenties, with bags upon bags filled with clothes that probably cost more than my yearly teaching salary. I was totally out of my element.

Natasha greeted me with a warm smile and a hug. "Nice to see you again, Shelby!" she said. "What kind of outfit are we in the market for? You have such a great figure. I think we should really accentuate it. Let's pull out all the stops tonight!"

"I don't know about that. I'm already pretty overwhelmed just by what I am seeing walking down this street," I replied. "I feel like all of these clothes will be way too expensive, and there is no way I'm going to find something to suit me."

"Don't be so negative! We've got you covered! We'll find something that's perfect for you, you will feel fantastic in, and will leave all the men drooling after you," Natasha said.

I rolled my eyes at that notion. I hadn't even thought about attracting another man. It felt like everything with Dave was still too fresh, and I didn't feel ready to journey down the road to my next relationship.

After shopping for a few hours, we settled upon a tight red cocktail dress that made me feel very self-conscious, but Natasha assured me that I looked stunning in it. We agreed to meet at a bar that catered more toward the 30-something crowd in an up-and-coming neighborhood of Los Angeles. When we arrived, people definitely took notice of Aiden and made a fuss to ensure we received a booth and a round of cocktails on the house. I felt nervous about being out at all, so I must have downed about five cocktails in the first hour.

Aiden, Natasha, and I were deep in a conversation that I wasn't paying much attention to (being completely three sheets to the wind at that point) when I suddenly noticed the most handsome man on the planet directly across the room from me. He was tall with an athletic frame, clean-shaven, and had dark blond hair that just barely draped over one of his eyes. And I couldn't help but notice the most intense blue eyes I had ever seen in my life. I felt like I recongnized him from somewhere.

"I think I have died and gone to heaven," I blurted out.

"What are you talking about?" asked Aiden.

Natasha looked in the same direction I was blatantly staring and noticed who I was talking about. "Oh my gosh! Isn't that Chris something? You know, the actor?" Natasha exclaimed.

"Oh, that's where I know him from!" I said. I had never seen such a gorgeous man up close and personal before.

"You should go over there and talk to him," Natasha suggested.

"What?! Me?!" I said, a little too loudly. "No way! There is no way a guy like that would be interested in me."

"Girl, do you even understand how good you look tonight? What have you got to lose?" she asked.

I thought about it for a minute. I did have quite a bit of liquid courage in me. What did I have to lose? It's not like I would ever see him again or get another opportunity like this.

"Okay. I'm going in," I said. It took me a minute to stand up and get my bearings.

"Are you sure you're in any kind of shape to be doing this?" asked Aiden.

"It's never or now," I stammered. Once I started walking, the effects of the alcohol seemed to come rushing in at once. I was starting to regret my decision to talk to the most gorgeous man in America in the state I was in. I slowly approached him and tried my best to act like I wasn't nearly as drunk as I was.

"Hello, there. I'm Shelby," I told him.

"Hi, Shelby. I'm Chris," he said, looking a little unsure about this strange woman who was suddenly approaching him. Luckily for me, it appeared that he had a few drinks in him as well.

"I'm a huge fan of yours, Chris. I just wanted to know if I could buy you a drink," I said.

"Sure. Why not?" he said. "I'll have a Scotch."

I motioned for the waitress to approach our table. "Two glasses of Glendronach 18, please," I ordered.

"You drink Scotch, too? You don't find many women who could handle a good Scotch," he told me.

"Well, I'm not like most women," I replied, flirtatiously.

"I can see that," said Chris. "Do you live in L.A., or are you just in town visiting?"

"I'm visiting to work on some songs in the studio with my friend over there," I motioned toward Aiden, who gave us a little wave.

"Aiden Jones, huh? He's got some good stuff," Chris said.

"We used to write songs together in college, but I took another career route and am now taking another shot at it," I told him.

"I'd love to hear some of your songs," said Chris.

"Why don't I sing one for you right now?" I replied. I casually leaned over and started singing seductively in his ear.

"I wanna feel your hand caress my skin.
I wanna kiss your lips and then begin,
To feel,
The love between you and me.

I wanna close my eyes and drift away.
I wanna fantasize and hear you say.
That you feel
The love between you and me.
Can you feel
The love between you and me?"

The next thing I knew, Chris was pulling me in towards him and kissing me passionately. Caught off guard, I realized this was the last thing I thought would happen. Once the initial shock wore off, though, I settled into the kiss. It had been so long since I had kissed anyone other than Dave, and it just dawned on me that I was currently kissing a man that most women would give their right kidney to be kissing. We continued kissing for what felt like hours when Chris suddenly pulled out of it.

"Wow, that was something else," he said. "You are quite the kisser, singer, and songwriter if I do say so myself."

"That kiss was definitely something," I replied. I was feeling much more sure of myself now and wanted to continue kissing, and possibly more, with Chris. I couldn't remember the last time I felt that alive and wanted. Maybe my libido hadn't died after all.

"I've got to get going. I have an early call time to set tomorrow," he said. "I've got to run to the restroom really quick, and then can I get your number?"

"Of course, you can," I replied, reeling in shock.

"Great. I'll be right back," he said.

As he made his way towards the bathrooms, I attempted to navigate my way back to the booth where Aiden and Natasha sat. They were both staring at me, mouths agape.

"I cannot believe what just happened," Natasha said. "I'm so jealous! Where did he go?"

"He just went to the restroom and then is going to get my number. He has an early call time tomorrow morning," I said, trying to fake a casualness as if this was something I said all the time. Then, I turned toward Natasha and changed my tune. "Can you believe I just made out with the most handsome man on the planet?"

"No, I cannot!" Natasha replied. "What was it like?"
"So, so good! I haven't kissed a man other than Dave in so long. I was afraid I wouldn't remember how to do it properly," I said.

Aiden was just staring at me with an expression I couldn't quite read. Before I knew it, Chris walked up behind me and gently touched my lower back.

"You two have a pretty talented friend, here," Chris said to Aiden and Natasha. "Not to mention the best kisser." He leaned in for another quick kiss. When he pulled away, I gave him my number and told him we'd be in touch.

After he left, I turned back to Aiden and Natasha. "No way is he ever going to call me, do you think?" I asked.

"He looked pretty enamored with you," Natasha said.

I was on such a high, I figured I should end the night while I was ahead. I said goodnight to Aiden and Natasha and caught a cab back to my hotel. I went to sleep with butterflies still fluttering in my stomach, wondering if I would ever see Chris again.

Chapter Ten

The next morning, I woke up for more studio time with the worst hangover of my life. Did what happened last night really happen I wondered, or was it all a dream? I thought back to the night before. I remembered lots of drinks and seeing a really handsome man, possibly kissing him. I couldn't be sure if it was all real.

When I got to the studio, I decided to ask Aiden.

"Well, if it isn't the seductress of the City of Angels," joked Aiden.

"What happened last night?" I asked in barely a whisper.

"You really don't remember making out with Hollywood's most eligible bachelor?" he asked.

"So that wasn't just a dream?" I asked. "I can't believe it!"

Suddenly there was a knock at the door, and a delivery man walked in with a huge bouquet of flowers. The card read, "I enjoyed getting to meet you last night. Here's hoping we have some more time together to "feel" each other out. Sincerely, Chris."

I couldn't believe my eyes. Was this really happening or was I living in a fairy tale?

"Looks like you made a good impression on him," said Aiden. "If you don't mind, I'd like to get on with our recording session. I am paying by the hour here." Aiden seemed a little perturbed at the flower delivery interruption.

"Of course," I said. "Sorry. I didn't know that would happen."

I stepped into the recording studio and downed a big gulp of my coffee to prepare myself for singing. I wasn't in the best shape, but I knew I still had to produce some high-quality stuff to make Aiden feel like he was getting his money's worth. I began singing.

"I saw you standing there.
I couldn't help but stare.
Your eyes they burned right through me.
There was no one else I could see.
And then you looked straight at me.
I fell so helplessly
In love with you.

There was nothing else I could do.
With your gorgeous eyes of blue.
They seemed to pierce through me.
You made me feel so free.
And then you looked straight at me.
I fell so helplessly
In love with you.

Oh, can't you see you're tearing me apart?
The way you pull at the strings of my poor heart.
Your smile lights up the room.
Oh, I can't help but swoon.

You started to walk towards me.

My head said please, please flee.
But my heart said don't go away.
I really beg you to stay.
And then you looked straight at me.
I feel so helplessly
In love with you.
In love with you.
In love with you."

I took off the headphones and stepped out of the studio to an annoyed look on Aiden's face. "That was great," he said. "But you have a visitor."

I turned to see Chris standing there in the studio.

"Hi, Shelby. That was some great stuff I just heard," he said.

"Chris! What are you doing here?" I asked.

"I just wanted to stop by and see if you wanted to go out for lunch," he said. "Did you get the flowers I sent?"

"Yes, I did. Thank you so much," I replied. I turned to Aiden. "Would it be okay to take a lunch break?"

"Sure, why not? I'll just work on some of the guitar and piano parts while you're gone," he said. "Nice to see you again, Chris." His face seemed more annoyed as time wore on.

"Are you sure? I don't want to leave if it's not okay with you. You are the one who is being so generous to me," I said. I didn't want to leave feeling like Aiden was mad at me.

"Yes, it's fine," he heaved a sigh. "Please, enjoy your lunch. We'll pick back up when you get back."

"Thanks so much, Aiden," I told him.

Chris took my arm in his. "Shall we?" he asked.

We walked out to a car parked outside, waiting for us. "Where are we going?" I asked.

"There's this great little cafe near here that I love to go to get a quick bite," he replied. "I have the afternoon off from shooting, so I figured I would surprise you and see if we could have a little lunch date. The studio provided this car and driver for me to get around."

"That is very kind of you," I told him. "You know, I really didn't think I was ever going to see you again."

"Are you crazy? After last night? I can't get you out of my head!" he told me.

I couldn't believe what I was hearing. Was this for real?

"I really enjoyed last night as well," I said. "Sorry if I came on a little strong. I might have had one too many drinks in me."

"Don't worry about that. Trust me, I have seen much worse," he said. "Here we are."

We arrived at the cafe, and the hostess showed us immediately to a table with no waiting. He had reserved a secluded spot away from the rest of the restaurant crowd. As we sat down, I figured I better start with some light conversation, since I had basically pounced on him immediately the night before.

"So, what kind of movie are you working on?" I asked.

"It's kind of a suspense/thriller type movie," he replied. "Have you seen many of my movies?"

"Yes, I've seen quite a few, but not all of them," I told him. "To be honest, I really like your comedic acting. I've heard that comedy is one of the toughest things to pull off, but I thought you did a great job with it. It must be difficult to be taken seriously with your acting when you are such a heartthrob." I smiled at him.

He laughed. "Yeah, I guess some places try to treat me as just eye candy, which is why I've been trying to take on some more serious roles."

"I've seen some of your serious work, too, which was great. You are a very versatile actor," I told him.

"You are quite the talented singer," he told me. "Why didn't you take on singing as a career like your friend Aiden?"

"I've always had a problem with singing in front of crowds," I told him. "I have dreamed of being a songwriter for so long, but it is difficult to get your songs out there if you aren't willing to sing them for people."

"You didn't have a problem singing one for me last night," he grinned at me flirtatiously.

"That was a different situation. I was very emboldened by alcohol," I told him, playfully.

"You don't have a problem singing in front of all those guys in the studio?" he asked.

"I've known Aiden for many years, so his presence kind of calms me," I answered. "If I'm in front of a big crowd, though, it wouldn't matter if someone was up there standing right next to me, I would still freak out."

"Well, I hope you get over that fear because I think you have a great singing voice," he told me.

"Thank you," I said. "I wish I could say that makes me feel better, but I am just really self-conscious. I'm kind of that way about everything. You wouldn't normally see me wearing a dress like the one I wore last night, either."

"You really have no idea how sexy you are, do you?" Chris asked.

I blushed. "Stop it. I am not," I replied.

"You know, your humility makes you even sexier," he said.

As self-conscious as I was, I still really enjoyed hearing those words from him. We enjoyed a delicious lunch and carried on a little bit longer with our chit-chat, discussing our families and our lives growing up, but before long I knew I had to get back to the studio or get an earful from Aiden.

"I better be getting back," I told Chris. "Aiden won't be happy if we don't get in the rest of the recording today. He's leaving for a tour in Europe in a couple of days, and we need to get everything done as soon as possible."

"I'm actually heading out of town tomorrow for a new shooting location," Chris said. "Would it be possible to get together tonight? I would love to hang out with you one last time before we part."

"That sounds great," I told him. "Just give me a call and let me know when and where."

Chris hopped back in the car with me and had his driver take me back to the studio. I felt like I was floating on Cloud Nine. Not only did I just have an amazing lunch date with an amazing man, but I also now had a night date planned with him as well. I didn't feel truly ready to make a commitment to another man, but this felt like a fun fling, and why wouldn't I take him up on his offer? Never in my wildest dreams did I think I would be dating a handsome Hollywood movie actor.

When I walked into the studio, Aiden was just finishing up the guitar part on a song.

"Hey, Shelby," he said, not appearing particularly happy. "How was your lunch date?"

"It was great!" I told him. "I haven't been on a date in so long, I almost forgot what it was like. We're going to get together again tonight."

"Oh, that's too bad. I was hoping you would want to hang out with Natasha and me tonight," Aiden said.

"Maybe the four of us can get together and do something," I told him.

"Yeah, maybe. I don't know what Mr. Hollywood has planned for the two of you, but I'm guessing it doesn't involve my wife and me," Aiden said.

"Oh, come on. We're just having fun. We both know we won't be seeing each other again after this," I said. "What song do you want me to work on now?"

"I think we have time for just one more," he said. "Are there any other really great songs you think will fit in well with the rest?"

"I have one more that I haven't shared with you yet. We can see what you think of it," I said.

"Okay. Let's have a listen," Aiden replied.

I went back into the studio and put on the headphones. For some reason, I was feeling particularly nervous about singing the next song, but I knew it would be a good fit. I wasn't sure how Aiden would react to it and hoped that he wouldn't read too much into it. I began to sing.

"Why do you burn me with those eyes?
Give me that feeling that I try so hard to disguise,
You know it feels so out of line.
Wish I could push you right out of my mind.

You know this feeling I feel
Is much too good to be real.
Why can't you just let me be?

I can't help this feeling I get.
You pull me in just like a magnet.
I try to get away 'cause I just cannot stay.
You keep pulling me in like a magnet.
Wish I could turn you off,
Like you keep turning me on.
Your force field is too strong.
Yeah,

Why do you speak to me that way?
Get me so focused on every word you say.
Wish I could taste those curvy lips,

And feel your hands across every inch of my skin.

But, no it just cannot be.
You are no good for me.
Why can't I just realize?

I can't help this feeling I get.
You pull me in just like a magnet.
I try to get away 'cause I just cannot stay.
You keep pulling me in like a magnet.
Wish I could turn you off,
Like you keep turning me on.
Your force field is just too strong.

I try, and I try, to pull away.
But no matter how hard I try I am completely consumed.
How can I be demagnetized?

I can't help this feeling I get.
You pull me in just like a magnet.
I try to get away 'cause I just cannot stay.
You keep pulling me in like a magnet.
Wish I could turn you off,
Like you keep turning me on.
Your force field is just too strong.
Yeah"

As soon as I stepped out of the studio, Aiden gave me a big grin.

"That sounds great. I think that's all we need for today," he told me. "Why don't you go back to your hotel and get ready for your big date tonight while I wrap things up here?"

He seemed to change his attitude quickly, which seemed strange. Maybe he was reading into the song. I hoped he hadn't guessed the meaning behind the song, but something told me that he did.

"And Shelby?" he asked.

"Yes?" I replied.

"I think Natasha and I would like to join you guys tonight if that's okay," he said. I was a little taken aback by that response.

"Sure thing. I will just check in with Chris and see what he has planned, but I'm sure it won't be a problem," I said.

"Great," said Aiden. "Looking forward to it." He gave me a very mischievous grin as I walked out the door to grab a cab to the hotel.

Chapter Eleven

Chris called me around 5 o'clock that afternoon. "Are we still on for tonight?" he asked.

"Of course!" I told him. "Although would you mind if my friend Aiden and his wife tagged along with us for a bit? They wanted to get together for our last night in Los Angeles."

"Sure, that's no problem. The more the merrier," said Chris.

Chris wouldn't tell me exactly what he had planned for the night, but he told me the address and that I should dress casually. I wasn't sure what he was up to, but I was already acting completely out of character, so why not just go all-in? Besides, I would have Aiden and Natasha there with me, so it wasn't like he was going to take me to a back alley and murder me or something. Aiden, Natasha, and I decided to all grab a cab together and arrived at the place right on time. It turned out to be a karaoke bar.

"Oh, geez," I said as we pulled up to the place.

"Maybe this Chris guy doesn't know you so well, huh?" Aiden remarked.

"Well, I did tell him that I didn't like singing in front of crowds, so I imagine he's trying to get me over that fear," I said.

"Good luck with that. I tried for several months, and look where that got us," Aiden said.

I felt hurt by his remark. He was so sure that he knew me so well. We hadn't seen each other in so many years, so who did he think he was judging me in that way? I felt more determined than ever to show Aiden that I was nothing like the young, mousy, shy girl he knew in college. After all, I was dating a movie star and even made out with him in public. I bet he didn't think I would be the type of person to do that either, right?

We walked in, and Chris got up from his seat at a table to greet us. He kissed me sweetly on the cheek. "Surprise!" he said. "This is one of my favorite karaoke bars. I hope your voice isn't too strained from the studio this week. I figured we could just kick back and have a little fun here. No pressure."

"Maybe no pressure for you, but Shelby doesn't exactly enjoy this type of thing," said Aiden.

"Maybe you should just let me speak for myself," I replied. "You don't know the first thing about my likes and dislikes." I knew I was being adamant just to prove Aiden wrong.

Chris went up to the bar to grab us some drinks. I was thankful that I would have a little liquid courage for the night. We sat and watched some middle-aged women sing 80's songs for a while before deciding to get up and check out the catalog.

"I hate to disappoint you all, but I cannot carry a tune," Natasha said. "I think all of the singing will be left to you three."

"No one's judging anyone's singing ability," said Chris. "Feel free to sing out loud and proud, even if you are off-key." He smiled at her, and she blushed. I felt a slight twinge of anger welling up inside of me. She already had Aiden, why did she have to flirt with Chris, too?

Chris asked me if I knew any Sinatra songs, and I told him yes. He picked us out a duet to ease me into the process. "You'll do great!"

Chris said. "This should be an easy one because both parts are singing the whole time, you'll just have the harmony."

"Thanks," I told him. "I just hope my nerves don't get the better of me."

We got up there and began to sing "Something Stupid" together. I had heard him sing before, but I was taken aback by how good he was live. He sounded just like Sinatra with his deep and sultry tone. I found myself even more entranced with him. I looked out to Aiden and Natasha as we sang. Aiden did not look impressed. When we finished, the audience clapped, and I felt my nerves dissipate a bit.

Next up on the mic was Aiden. He had chosen the Beatles' "Can't Buy Me Love" and of course did an amazing rendition of the song. Singing seemed to come so easily to Aiden and being on stage looked just as comfortable to him as if he was sitting at home watching television. I wished I had that kind of confidence and comfort while on stage. When Aiden was done, he came back to the table and asked me if I was ready to sing one by myself.

"Yes, I think that's a great idea!" said Chris. "You have such a great voice. I would love to hear one with just you if you don't mind."

"Well, I suppose I could," I said. I downed the rest of my drink and went to the song catalog. I figured my safest bet would be a well-known song in a lower register to best combat my nerves. I stepped up the microphone to sing "(They Long to Be) Close to You" by the Carpenters. As I sang, I tried my hardest not to let my nerves get the best of me. I decided the best way to do that was to focus on my table only and ingnore all of the other eyes staring at me from the audience. I found myself drifting between looking at Chris and looking at Aiden. I thought to myself how true the words were that I was currently singing. Here I was, at a karaoke bar, with two gorgeous men that any woman would be dying to be near. Bothof these guys had women vying for their attention at all times and fantasizing about them at any given moment of the day. I kept staring from one set of blue eyes to the other, wondering how I had gotten so lucky. What was so special about me to have both these amazing guys in my life? I tried to focus my attention on Chris to let him know how interested I was and that his flirty looks were not going unnoticed, but for some reason, I kept drifting more towards Aiden. He had a longing look in his eyes, and I found myself longing for him as well. If only we could be as close as we used to be. I hoped that Natasha had not noticed my unintentional staring in his direction.

When the song was over, Chris gave me a standing ovation, and Aiden called for an encore. I had done it. I had performed by myself on a stage in front of a large crowd of people and made it out alive. I hadn't even felt that nervous, and my voice didn't get shaky like I had worried it might. Looking out at Aiden had calmed my nerves in the same way he calmed me in the studio and while we were writing songs together. I couldn't explain the reason for the effect he had on me, but he always made me feel comfortable and safe.

After several more drinks, some pizza, and a few more songs, Aiden and Natasha said that they had to leave because Natasha had an early flight in the morning, and Aiden had to get things ready for his tour. Chris and I both decided to stay for some more drinks, and a little while later, he invited me back to his place.

I hadn't really considered this possibility, but I thought I would be crazy not to accept his invitation. I looked around the room at all the women watching us and recognized the longing in their eyes. This whole trip was so far out of my comfort zone that I didn't think I would ever be the same again. Needless to say, I took Chris up on his offer.

We got in his car and made the long drive out to his secluded spot in Beverly Hills. His place wasn't the huge mansion I had imagined in my mind, but it was a nice spot away from the busyness of the main part of the neighborhood. With a screen of trees, it didn't feel like we were surrounded by other million-dollar houses at all.

Chris invited me in and asked if I wanted a glass of wine. I was already so many drinks in, but I knew if I was going to do what I really wanted to do with him tonight, I would need the aphrodisiac effect that wine had on me. He poured me a glass of port, which just happened to be my drink of choice to get me in the mood.

We sat down on his plush couch and chatted for a bit when the conversation inevitably turned physical. He tilted his head and kissed me gently as I relaxed into the temptation. I knew I was still a little tipsy, but I made sure this time that I didn't drink so much that I wouldn't remember the next day. I wanted this night burned in my memory forever. I knew another night like one wasn't likely to come along in my lifetime.

We leaned back onto the couch, and his hands were moving all around my back as his lips made their way down my neck. His lips and tongue explored every inch of my neck and chest. As Chris worked his way down to my breasts, shivers of electricity and anticipation traveled down my spine. I sat up and whipped my shirt off over my head as he did the same. We continued kissing as our hands trailed over each other's bodies, but then he whispered in my ear asking if I wanted to go to the bedroom. I whispered back "yes" and felt like we couldn't get there quick enough.

We made love for hours and hours, and I never wanted to stop. I had never felt more aroused or alive. I felt like I was living in some kind of fantasy world. It seemed like we were acting out all the best love scenes from all of the most romantic movies. If this is what it was like being with an actor, I never wanted to go back. It was like he knew all the best moves to make and all of the spots on my body that would make me moan with delight and beg for more. I didn't want to think about how much practice he might have had. I just wanted to revel in every delicious moment.

I don't know what time I fell asleep, but I awoke the next morning in his soft, plush bed to the smell of bacon and coffee. I felt like

I was still dreaming. I felt the inclination to pinch myself before getting out of bed. This kind of thing did not happen to women like me. Who did I think I was? I was just a mom, teacher, and former wife. Here I was, living life like some kind of supermodel, sleeping with the best-looking man I'd ever laid eyes on.

I walked into the kitchen and saw Chris stirring some scrambled eggs in a pan, wearing nothing but his boxers. The muscles in his toned back rippled with each movement. I just wanted to stand there and watch him all morning, admiring this beautiful creature that God sent down directly from heaven.

He turned around and noticed me staring, "Well, good morning! I hope you're hungry. I know I am after the night we had."

"Is this for real?" I asked.

"Well, it's not exactly a gourmet meal, but I tried my best," Chris said.

"I mean, how did I get to be so lucky? What did I do to deserve all of this?" I asked.

"You deserve much more than this. I am the lucky one. I wish you knew just how amazing you really are," he replied.

I felt like I had wandered into some sort of an alternate reality, but I didn't want it to end, so I decided to just go along with it like this was an everyday occurrence. We sat down to enjoy our breakfast when I got a call from Aiden.

"Hello?" I answered.

"Shelby, guess what? I secured a place for you on my European tour. You can be my opener!" he said.

"Wait, what!?" I asked. I couldn't believe what I was hearing. Was he really expecting me to leave with him on a trip to Europe at a moment's notice? "What are you talking about? I can't just go with you to Europe!"

"Of course, you can! I already talked with your mom about it," Aiden said. "She's going to take care of the kids and make sure they get to school in time and everything else. It is already arranged."

"But I would still want to see my kids before I go," I told him. "I have never been away from them for this long, and now you want me to be gone for months at a time?"

"It would only be for two weeks. You would only be on the first leg of the tour," Aiden said. "You would be coming along with me to London, Madrid, Rome, Milan, Paris, Berlin, and Athens. It's already arranged. You can fly back home for a couple of days and then meet me in London."

"But I haven't prepared or practiced or anything! What on earth am I going to sing, and how am I going to sing in front of a big crowd of people?" I asked him.

"I think you proved last night that you are perfectly capable of singing in front of a crowd," he said. "C'mon, I had to pull a lot of strings to get everyone to agree to do this. Don't back out on me now."

"But I never agreed to this in the first place!" I couldn't believe what I was hearing. How could he just assume that I would be okay with this?

"Shelby, I'll be there with you every step of the way. If you get nervous, I'll calm your nerves. I'll help you practice along the way. I'm not going to let you do all of this on your own," Aiden said.

Suddenly, Chris interjected. "Shelby, is everything okay?"

"Who is that? Is that Chris?" Aiden asked.

"Ummm..." I didn't quite know how to respond.

"Did you spend the night with him last night?" Aiden didn't seem happy about this new development.

"That's really none of your business," I told him in the calmest tone I could muster. I was feeling a little ashamed of myself and didn't want to feel like I was disappointing Aiden too. "You know what, Aiden? Okay. I will go with you."

His disapproving tone turned to one of enthusiasm. "That's great news! I'll get the ball rolling, then. You won't be disappointed. I think you are really going to enjoy being on the road, Shelby," Aiden said.

"Let's hope you're right," I replied. I hung up the phone and turned to Chris.

"What was that all about?" Chris asked.

"Aiden asked me to go on the first leg of his European tour with him," I told him.

"I bet he did," said Chris.

"What's that supposed to mean?" I asked him.

"Aiden just seems very protective of you, like he wants you all to himself," Chris said. "I see the way he looks at you. His wedding band may indicate marriage, but it seems to me he only has eyes for you."

"That's ridiculous," I told him. "Aiden and I haven't been together in years. He is obviously head over heels in love with Natasha."

"You can keep telling yourself that all you want, but his actions tell another story," Chris said. "Why do you think he's jumping through all of these hoops for you? Does he go to such these great lengths for all of his friends?"

I gave some thought to what Chris was telling me. Was Aiden just doing all of this as a friend who wants to see his friend succeed, or was there more to the story than he was letting on?

Chapter Twelve

Even though I was tempted to stay in that kitchen with Chris all day, I eventually pried myself away from him to get back to my hotel room for checkout. I gave my mom a call as I was on my way to the airport.

"Hey, Mom. How is everything going with the kids?" I asked.

"Oh, everything is great, dear! We're having so much fun together. It's nice having little ones around the house all the time again," she said.

"Mom, did Aiden call you and talk to you about the tour?" I asked.

"Yes, he did, and I think it is such a great idea! Isn't this what you have always dreamed of? Getting your music career off and running? It sounds like a wonderful tour to be a part of as well. Just imagine all the places you'll get to see! I'm so jealous!" she sounded genuinely excited for me.

"But won't it be too much extra work for you? I feel like I'm just dumping the kids off on you and expecting you to raise them. I feel like I'm neglecting my mommy duties," I told her.

"Don't you worry about the kids. They're holding up just fine, and we'll make sure to keep in touch with you while you're gone," Mom said.

"Okay, if, you're sure. Can I talk to them now?" I asked.

"Sure. Here's Billy," Mom said.

"Hey, Mom. How's L.A.?" Billy asked.

"Hey, Sweetie. L.A. has been a lot of fun, but I really miss you guys. How have things been going for you there?" I asked him.

"Really good. Grandma is the best cook, so we are eating some awesome dinners," he informed me. "No offense, Mom. We really miss you, though."

I laughed. "No offense taken. I know Grandma's cooking is second-to-none. Are you two getting along okay and making sure to get all your work done and help around the house?"

"Yeah. Grandma has a scheduled time for us to do homework every day. and we both have assigned chores to do, too. We've been learning some fun card games that we play together," Billy said.

"That's great, Honey! You 'll have to show those to me some time," I told him. "Can you put your sister on the phone so I can talk to her, too?"

"Sure, Mom. Love and miss you!" he said.

"Love and miss you too!" I told Billy.

"Hi, Mommy!" Bonnie said enthusiastically as she answered the phone. "I miss you!"

"Hi, Sweetheart! Mommy misses you too!" I was trying desperately not to let the tears come in, but I found myself getting emotional talking to them. "Are you having fun with Grandma?"

"Yeah! We've been making homemade cookies today! They taste so yummy!" Bonnie said.

"That's fantastic! Do you think you'll be okay if Mommy travels for a bit longer? I sure do miss you two!" I told her.

"I will miss you, but we're having a lot of fun with Grandma," she said. "Are you having fun too, Mommy?"

"I am having fun, too. I'm going to have all kinds of new music for you and your brother to listen to when I come back. I was in a real recording studio and everything!" I told Bonnie.

"That does sound like fun! I can't wait to hear what you did," she said.

"I can't wait either! I better go now, Honey. I'm at the airport now. I'm going to fly home for a few days before I go to Europe. I'll see you soon, I promise!" I told her.

"Okay, Mommy! See you soon!" she hung up the phone.

I couldn't believe how resilient my kids were being. They seemed to be coping just fine with my mom. Maybe even better than they were before since they didn't have parents who were constantly screaming at each other. I couldn't wait to get back and see them for a bit before heading out on tour.

The thought that I would be going on tour suddenly hit me like a Mack truck. How can I be about to embark on a European tour with Aiden? Just a few short months ago, I had given up my dream of being a songwriter and was just focusing on being a teacher. It seemed my life had done a complete 180 in a very short period. It's crazy what types of curveballs life can throw at you sometimes.

After I made my way through security and found my gate, I gave Aiden a call.

"Well, I called my mom and kids, and I guess I'm going through with this," I told him.

"That's great news! See, you have nothing to worry about. This tour is really going to be great for your songwriting career, you'll see. Those people have no idea of what talent is headed their way. I can't wait to hear you perform your songs on stage," Aiden said.

"Yeah, about that...Do you really think I'll be fine, and my stage fright won't get the best of me?" I asked him.

"After seeing you perform in karaoke, it seemed like you had a newfound confidence. It seems like the old, shy Shelby has gone away and a new, confident Shelby has taken her place," Aiden said.

"Really? I didn't get that feeling at all. Maybe I was trying to impress Chris to make myself feel like I really deserved a shot with him," I said.

"What about Chris? Are you in a relationship with him now or what? I don't think it's the greatest idea to get involved in a relationship if you are about to go out on a tour," he said.

I sensed a slight twinge of jealousy in his tone of voice. "Chris and I aren't in a relationship. He was just a fun fling. I'm still in shock that anything even happened with him. I really didn't think I had a shot in hell," I said.

"You really don't know just how fantastic you are, do you?" Aiden asked me.

"What do you mean by that?" I asked.

"Nothing. Maybe you will realize it one day," Aiden said. "I better go. I need to wrap up a few things here at the studio today to finish mixing the record. I hope you enjoy your time together with your family. I'll meet you in London!"

"Sounds great! Good luck with the record!" I told him. I hung up the phone but began to wonder if some of what Chris shared about Aiden might be right.

Chapter Thirteen

The next few days were a complete blur. I couldn't seem to sit still. I had millions of thoughts running through my mind. I was starting to get anxious and excited all at the same time.

When departure day finally came, it was much more difficult than I had imagined. I had just come back from being away from my kids for a few days and that was hard enough. How was I going to cope with being gone for a couple of weeks? I knew my mom was a pro and would be just fine, but I was more worried about how I was going to cope. What if I broke down crying in the middle of a performance? What if my stage fright reared its ugly head again and I freeze up on stage? All my past concerns and fears starting welling up inside of me again.

As soon as the taxi pulled up, I turned to my mom. "Mom, I don't know if I can go through with this," I told her.

"Don't be silly, Honey. You're going to be great!" she replied.

"How can you be so sure? I've never done anything like this in my life! This isn't me. I'm just a normal woman who does normal stuff. Who do I think I am embarking on a European tour with a well-known musician? This doesn't feel like it's real."

"Honey, just because it doesn't feel real doesn't mean it's not. Sometimes life can throw things at you that you just don't expect. That doesn't mean it's a bad thing. When your biggest dream in life comes true, you don't run for the hills. You tackle it head-on," Mom said.

I took a big exhale. "You're right, Mom. There's no way I can be a real songwriter if I don't get my songs out there for people to hear. I never wanted to be the one center stage receiving all of the attention, but if that's what it takes to get my voice heard, so be it."

"That's the spirit! Now go out there and have fun living your life!" Mom gave me a huge hug and opened the door for me. "Call us when you get to London and let us know how fabulous it is!"

"Will do, Mom. Billy! Bonnie! Mommy's leaving!" I called to the kids.

"Bye Mommy!" they yelled in unison as they ran to hug me goodbye.

As I climbed into the taxi, I sat in stunned silence, taking in everything that was happening in my life. For so many years, I had dreamed of being a songwriter, and now that it was actually happening. It felt like I was living someone else's life. After the huge meltdown of a year I had experienced, I was glad things were starting to look up for me. Sure, things were a little complicated. I was on tour with my ex, but at least it wasn't some stranger I would be traveling with. It was comforting to know Aiden was going to be along with me for this ride. Despite everything that had happened between us, he still had a calming presence that I hadn't felt with any other boyfriend, or friend for that matter.

On the plane, I began to daydream about my time in L.A. with Chris. What a whirlwind few days that was! I was still in shock thinking about how lucky I had been to get to spend that time with him. Sure, I had a crush on him from seeing his movies, but to get to spend the night with him? No way in a million years did I think that would happen!

Thinking back to that night inspired me to write a song on the plane. Even just writing it and remembering those feelings got me all hot and bothered. I hoped the other passengers couldn't tell the kinds of thoughts that were running through my head! I started remembering slow dancing in the middle of the night, and the words started flowing out:

I see your body sway to a brand-new beat.
My body starts to move, can't control my feet.
You pull me in close, your hand touches mine.
Don't know what happened next, lost all track of time.

Chorus:
I wanna do more than dance with you baby, dance with you baby.
So won't you come on over here, you're driving
me crazy, driving me crazy.
I wanna feel your hands all over me.
You better get ready.
I'm really gonna rock your world.
Yeah Ohhhh,
I'm really gonna rock your world.
Ohhh Ohhhh.

The next thing I hear, "Does this feel okay?"
My heart starts racing, my mind's gone away.
The smell of your cologne is getting me high.
I could stay like this the rest of the night.

Chorus

Bridge:
Can we move this off of the dance floor?
My mind is saying no, but my body is wanting more…

Chorus

As soon as I finished writing the lyrics, I closed my eyes and started fantasizing about being back at Chris's. I could still feel his strong hands on me and see those intense blue eyes looking at me like they were taking in every part of my soul.

The next thing I knew, we were landing at Heathrow Airport. *Whew,* I thought, *I'm going to need to take a cold shower as soon as I check in to my room!*

When I stepped out of the gate, I was shocked to see Aiden standing there with a bouquet of flowers.

"What are you doing here?" I asked him. "I thought I wouldn't see you until later at rehearsal."

"I just wanted to show up personally and apologize for my actions," he said. "I know I didn't exactly go about this situation in the best way, and I realize I came on a bit strong and maybe made you feel like you were forced into this. I'm really sorry."

I couldn't believe I was getting this kind of apology from him. When he took off for Nashville in college, I was so desperate for him to apologize for so many years and it never happened. Now it was happening with no prompting whatsoever. I guess people really can change.

"There's no apology necessary," I told him. "I really needed that push to find out if I could do this. I've dreamt about it for so long, but I've been so afraid to put myself out there. I'm so terrified that people will think that I'm not talented enough or that I'm just singing songs that they've heard before."

"Are you kidding?" Aiden asked. "You're one of the most talented people I've ever met! If I didn't think so, I wouldn't have basically begged you to come out on tour with me."

"Well, I don't know if you really begged me," I said. "On second thought, I could do with a little more begging. Would you mind putting a little more effort into it?" I smirked at him.

Aiden got down on his knees in the middle of the airport and started exclaiming loudly. "Shelby! Will you please do me the honor of coming out on tour with me?!"

I turned bright red. "Aiden, I was just joking. You really didn't have to do that.

"I know," he said. "But I do so enjoy embarrassing you and making you feel uncomfortable." He smiled.

He walked along with me through the airport, and we got into a cab together.

"So," I asked him, "Are we staying in hotels the whole time, or am I going to get to experience the thrill of sleeping on a tour bus?"

"Sorry to disappoint you, but for this leg of the tour, we are sleeping in hotels. Trust me, you are better off," Aiden smiled again. I had forgotten how much I enjoyed seeing him smile. Whenever Aiden sang, he always looked very serious and intensely focused on the music he was playing and the lyrics he was singing. He had such a gentle, soulful smile, and it was a refreshing change to see it more and more.

When the taxi dropped us off, Aiden left me to check into my room. "Soundcheck is at 2, and the doors will open for the show at 6:30," he said. "You should bring a change of clothes with you to soundcheck, because you won't have time to come back here and change. Whatever you want to wear for the show, including makeup and hair accessories, should come with you."

"Look at you, all of a sudden so interested in hair, makeup, and fashion," I teased him.

"I'm not really, but it kind of comes with the territory," he said. "I'm always more concerned about how many shirts I'm going to sweat through in one night and if I have a whiskey for after the show to numb my sore throat."

"Gotcha," I said. I settled into my room and began to decide options for what to wear during the concert. I also had to go through my setlist and figure out what I would play and in what order. Aiden had told me that I would have one guy as backup on guitar, but other than that I was pretty much on my own.

As I headed out for the soundcheck, I kept checking and re-checking the details to make sure I had everything in order just the way I wanted it. I couldn't control what was going to happen to me as I performed that night. However, if I could get a handle on the organization part, I could feel a little bit better about the situation.

When we arrived at the venue I had to do a double-take. I couldn't believe how massive it was! I thought we would just be playing smaller venues, maybe some larger bars, but nothing like what stood in front of me at that moment. I fetl the panic starting to well up inside of me, and there wasn't even a crowd there yet.

I took my guitar out of the cab and headed toward the back entrance where the bands entered the concert hall. Aiden spotted me and came over to greet me with a hug. "You made it!" he said.

"Yeah, I wasn't sure the guy drove me to the right place," I said. "This place is so huge!"

"Yeah, for the European tours, they tend to get a little bit larger venues because we don't come over here as often. We can usually fill them up easier than we can in the States," Aiden said.

"Well, a little bit of a warning would have been nice," I told him.

"Sorry, I didn't even think about it being an issue. Are you okay?" he asked, looking concerned.

"I guess I'll have to be, won't I?" I replied. I gave him what I hoped was a reassuring smile. "I'll just pretend they're all in their underwear or something. Does that trick really work?"

"Not really," Aiden said. "But if it helps, you really can't see any of the people past the first three rows. Just imagine you are playing for those people only and ignore all of the other people in the venue."

"Thanks," I told him. I hoped that strategy would help.

I set up on the stage for the soundcheck and met the man who would be my guitar backup for the tour. He assured me that he had been rehearsing my songs but would go along with whatever changes I wanted to make. I was grateful he was so easygoing about it.

I sat down on a stool and started tuning my guitar. As soon as I heard the echo of it ringing through the giant hall, I started feeling a little queasy. Then I began singing my first song and couldn't remember all the words in the first verse. Everything sounded so loud, and I kept looking around at all the empty seats and imagining them all being filled with people later that night. Suddenly, the whole room began to spin. I felt myself falling over, and everything went black.

Chapter Fourteen

"Shelby? Shelby, are you okay?" I could hear Aiden asking me as if from a great distance.

I blinked my eyes open and realized I was laying down on a stage. "What happened?" I asked him.

"I guess you passed out," Aiden replied. "Shelby, if this is too much pressure for you, please just let me know. You really don't have to do this."

"No, it's okay," I said. "I think I just got overwhelmed for a minute. I'll be okay. Everyone went through so much work to get this together; I don't want to ruin it for everyone."

"Are you sure? I feel horrible that this happened to you," Aiden said. He looked so concerned and cared so much about my well-being, that my heart softened a little.

"I am sure. I don't know what happened, but I can handle it," I said, smiling at him.

I sat back down on the stool and tried to pick up right where I'd left off. I closed my eyes and imagined the entire place filled but started feeling queasy again. I opened my eyes and took a deep breath. Then, I closed my eyes again and saw Aiden's face. He was looking me in the eyes and telling me I could do it. He smiled in that reassuring way of his. I opened my eyes and looked over at him. He still looked concerned that I was about to pass out again. I took another deep breath and started playing the intro to my song.

"I looked in your eyes and then something grabbed me.
Could this really be what I think it could be?
I know you can't see it, but I know I can feel it.
There's something between you and me.
Chorus:
Tell me why, when I look in your eyes
I see so many great things about you.
Why can't you feel the same way too?
Tell me why am I falling in love with you?

You push me away when I try to get near.
Can't you see I'm so lonely without you here?
You think it's not right, but just give it a try.
There's no part of love to fear.

Chorus

I know you can't see it, but I know I can feel it.
There's something between you and me.

Chorus

As I finished the song, I looked back over to Aiden and saw him staring intently at me. A warm feeling rushed through me, and I thought for a minute I was going to pass out again, but then I realized that wasn't what I was feeling. I had to look away from Aiden and focus instead on the next song we would be sound checking.

"That sounded great!" said Greg, my backup guitarist.

I snapped out of my reveries. "Thanks," I replied.

"Just one more to check, then?" he asked me.

"Yes, just one more," I said. I looked back over at Aiden, and he was still staring at me. I had to force myself to look away. I wasn't sure what was happening, but I knew that if it continued, it would be bad news for both of us.

We finished our sound check, and then Aiden's band set up to do his soundcheck. I stayed as far away from Aiden as possible. A part of me told me to get as close to him as possible since he gave me that feeling of comfort that I so desperately needed at that moment, but another part of me said that if I stayed close to him, we would probably do something we'd both regret.

After Aiden finished his soundcheck, he came backstage to talk to me. "Hey, Shelby," he said.

"Oh, hey, Aiden," I said as nonchalantly as possible. "How did your soundcheck go?"

"Everything sounds great so far," he replied. "Listen, Shelby. Do you think it's a bad idea for us to be on tour together?" "What do you mean?" I asked him, pretty sure I already knew the answer.

"I mean with our history. Aren't you afraid that some old feelings may resurface while we're spending all of this time together?" he asked.

"No, I think it will be fine," I lied. Then I added, "If you were worried about that happening, why did you invite me on this tour with you?"

Aiden stared at me for a long time before providing his answer. "Honestly, I was just excited to be around someone who understood me again." He looked away from me. "It gets pretty lonely when you are out doing this on your own. Natasha doesn't understand the music business and all of the stress that goes along with it. She also doesn't understand the creative part of the process and all the solitude that it requires. She just wants to talk nonstop whenever I'm around her, and I can't get anything accomplished. Sometimes I go on trips by myself just so I can get away and focus on my own creativity. I need to block out the noise sometimes, you know?"

"I do know," I told him. "I have two kids, remember? Why do you think I haven't written anything in so long?" I smiled at him.

"I guess you do know," he smiled back at me. "She just gets angry with me when I need time by myself. She is very extroverted, and I guess I just can't relate. I need to have time to just go inside my head and think. Maybe that's why they say, 'opposites attract' right?" He looked at me and seemed a little unsure of himself.

"That's true, to some degree," I said. "My husband and I were quite the opposites. Sometimes you need someone like you who can really understand what you are going through though, don't you?"

"Exactly," Aiden said. "That's why I was so grateful that we became friends again. It'as nice to have someone like-minded around." He smiled at me again. "I just want you to know how much I appreciate you being here. Sorry, I turned this into some kind of therapy session. I guess I've just had a lot on my mind lately."

I smiled at him again. "It's okay. Like you said, it's nice to have someone around who understands. Although, I don't think you can ever understand my tremendous stage fright. What if I pass out during the concert tonight?"

"I'll be right here. Just look over at me and focus on me, not on the crowd," he said. "If you start falling again, I'll be right there to help you back up."

I was so thankful he told me that. I still couldn't shake the nerves, but somehow knowing he would be there the whole time did make me feel more comfortable. I didn't know why he had that effect on me. Maybe it was just because we knew each other for so long and understood each other so well. I knew this was a fear I had to overcome if I was ever going to become a songwriter.

Aiden left my dressing room to get ready for the concert, and I sat there looking over my setlist for a while, beginning to second-guess some of my choices. I had mostly original songs but threw in a few covers to balance things out, since no one there would have ever heard of me. I kept telling myself that they were there to see Aiden, not me, so it really didn't matter what I did tonight.

Later that night, I peered out from behind the curtain and looked out at the crowd. It was a packed house, just as Aiden had predicted. I tried to keep taking deep breaths and just focus on the music I would be playing rather than the gigantic crowd of people looming before me.

Greg came up behind me and said, "You ready to go? I think we have about five minutes until showtime."

"I guess I'm as ready as I'll ever be," I replied.

I took one last look in the mirror to make sure I looked halfway decent when I noticed Aiden walking up behind me. He was wearing his usual concert attire of tight-fitting black pants and a white, body-hugging t-shirt. The ladies always loved that look on him. I noticed that he was freshly shaven, and his hair fell gently into his eyes in a playful way.

"Ready to go?" he asked me. "You look beautiful, by the way."

"Thank you," I replied. "I suppose I'm ready to go. I just really hope my nerves don't get the best of me."

"Just remember, I'll be right here," he said.

"Thanks again," I said. "That really helps. It's nice to have a friendly face nearby for the most terrifying moment of my life."

He laughed. "It won't be that terrifying, I promise. After this first concert, you'll be just fine. Even after the first song. The nerves will go away quickly. Now, go out there and break a leg."

"I'll try," I told him. I took a deep breath and prepared myself to walk out onto the scariest stage I had ever seen.

As I stepped into the middle of the stage, I introduced myself and sat down to play my first song. I started feeling the nerves climbing again the second I started playing the first note, so I looked over to the backstage area. Sure enough, Aiden was standing right there with that reassuring smile of his. He looked so proud watching me begin to play. I instantly felt more relaxed as I started singing. Every time I started feeling those nervous butterflies, I would just look over to Aiden, and he would be there. He watched me perform every single song from the same spot backstage. As I finished up my last song, I looked over and could've sworn I saw him get a little teary-eyed. I smiled at him and then smiled and waved at the audience, thanking them. To my surprise, a thunderous wave of applause washed over me. I wasn't sure if it was because I was done and they knew they were closer to seeing Aiden perform, or if they really enjoyed my performance. Either way, the feeling I experienced while leaving that stage made me remember why I enjoyed doing this in the first place. It was all about getting my music out there. It was my own kind of therapy. Maybe they just liked the melody, maybe they just liked the lyrics, or maybe they liked both. Either way, they were listening to what I had to say and taking note that I was here to stay.

Chapter Fifteen

After putting my guitar away, I came back towards the stage to watch Aiden's set. I had forgotten how magnetic he could be on the stage. He took command of the entire stage as if he owned it and owned everyone who watched him as well. During some songs he stood in the middle of the stage and played his guitar, but for other songs he would strut around on the stage slapping girls' hands as he passed by. You could hear the squeals of the girls who had just touched his coveted hand. Some girls screamed, some girls cried, and some just seemed mesmerized by the gorgeous man with the gorgeous voice standing in front of them. It was amazing to see how captivating he could be.

As one of the more up-tempo songs ended, the rest of his band left the stage, and Aiden sat on a stool in the middle of the stage with an acoustic guitar. Aiden told the crowd that he was going to take it down a notch with a ballad. He rarely did covers anymore since he had become such a huge star and everyone knew his songs, but he said that he was going to perform one of his favorite love songs for everyone.

Aiden sat down and began playing the first few notes of a love song I knew well. It was "Please Forgive Me" by Bryan Adams. As he began singing, he glanced over in my direction, and we locked eyes for what felt like an eternity. By the time he reached the end of the first chorus, as soon as he sang the words "please forgive me, I can't stop loving you" I turned and bolted to my dressing room. I could feel the tears welling up in my eyes. I didn't know what had come over me.

It had been so long since I had allowed myself to have those feelings for Aiden. I had been married for years, had an amazing, albeit short-lived, fling with a heartthrob actor, and yet for some reason, Aiden exerted a sort of power over me. It seemed like he could see straight into my soul. It made me feel both uncomfortable and at ease, both wrong and right. No one else ever came close to making me feel that way.

I knew Aiden always had a way of saying things through music that he could never really say through regular words, but I wasn't sure if this song was supposed to have some sort of secret meaning. Was there some kind of code I was supposed to be cracking? Does this mean he sees me as more than just a friend? And why on earth was I crying about it? I didn't want to stick around to find out.

I packed up everything I had in my dressing room and hailed a cab to my hotel room. We were supposed to get together for an after-party after the concert, but I felt like I couldn't be around Aiden after that. Some force was pulling me to him, but I did'ot want to be a homewrecker. Maybe I was just reading too much into it. There was something about the way that song and how he sang it while staring straight at me. It made me feel like there was definitely something he wasn't telling me.

When I got to the hotel, I immediately doused myself in a hot shower and crawled into bed to read my book. This was definitely not a night that I needed to get myself into trouble. I had the rest of the tour to think about. I needed to keep the focus on performing my songs and tackling my stage fright. I wanted to keep the focus on getting my songs out there, not on whatever I may or may not be feeling for my married ex-boyfriend.

At around midnight, Aiden called me. "Shelby? Where did you go?" he asked.

"Oh, hey Aiden. I was just really tired and worn out from a long night. I just wanted to get back to the hotel and get some rest," I lied.

"Oh, okay then," I could tell that he was disappointed. "I was just really looking forward to celebrating your first concert with you. You did such a great job!"

"Thanks, Aiden," I was starting to feel guilty for ditching him. "I'm sorry. I just needed to get out of there. I want to stay focused on the next concert and make sure I can keep my composure."

"I understand," he replied. "Maybe we can have a little celebration after the next concert, then."

"That sounds good," I said. "Maybe I'll feel a little more settled and used to everything by then."

I hung up the phone and tried to settle back into bed and get some rest, but I knew what I was going to be thinking about for the rest of the night. I only had one thing on my mind for the rest of the night, and that was Aiden. Somehow, I needed to find a way to push all thoughts and feelings of him aside. I'd done it once, and I was prepared to do it again.

Chapter Sixteen

The next morning, I convinced myself that my sole focus was going to be on my music and not passing out in front of this next crowd in Madrid. I met Aiden in front of the hotel to hop in the cab for our trip to the airport. He looked pretty groggy for our early morning flight.

"Long night last night?" I teased him.

"Yeah, these English people can really hold their liquor," he said. "I may have had just a few too many pints, and I definitely had too many shots of whiskey."

I giggled at him. "Are you going to be able to survive the car ride and the plane ride?"

"Yeah, I think so. Rock and roll, right?" he said as he placed his sunglasses back on his face and sunk into the back seat of the cab. Even though it was clear he was hungover and smelled vaguely of whiskey, he still had that clean, woodsy scent about him that I used to be unable to resist.

No! You're starting up already! My brain warned me. I needed to get my mind off of Aiden and focus on what why I was there.

"Oh, by the way," Aiden said. "I have a little surprise for you when we arrive in Madrid."

"What's that?" I asked.

"Oh, you'll see," he said as he gave me a little smirk and laid his head back down on the seat to take a nap the rest of the way to the airport.

Just great. Now I was starting to worry that my notions had been true, and he still had some lingering feelings for me. Doesn't matter. I needed to focus. I took out my book and tried to focus on the story, but it didn't seem to help. The book was about a boyfriend and girlfriend who had lost touch over the years and found their way back to each other. *Why on earth did I choose this book to read?* I wondered to myself. If I didn't watch it, I was in danger of becoming one of those romance book cliches. I looked over at Aiden, who was peacefully sleeping off his hangover. *How on earth does he look so good when he is hungover?* I wondered. *At least his eyes are covered by those sunglasses,* I thought, *but his hair is perfectly tousled, his curvy lips are parted just so...I must stop.* I decided it was best to stare out the window instead.

When we arrived at the airport, Aiden woke up like he had just received a second wind. "Ready to go?" he asked.

"How can you be so refreshed after that big hangover and short nap?" I asked him.

"Once you've done this for as long as I have, you develop a tolerance to this kind of thing," he said smiling at me.

We walked through the airport, and I couldn't help but notice all the stares Aiden received. I couldn't imagine what it was like to not be able to walk anywhere without being recognized. He just kept walking like nothing was even happening. He just stared straight ahead and acted like he was any regular person walking through the airport. At least I was getting through without anyone giving me a second glance.

We boarded the plane, and I realized that we were seated next to each other in first class. I had never flown first class before, so I was interested to see what it would be like.

"These seats are huge!" I exclaimed. "This is so great. I don't have to worry about some stranger bumping knees with me, or sneaking by me to go to the bathroom, or trying to hog the armrest, or falling asleep on my shoulder!"

Aiden laughed. "I guess I forgot all about that. You get kind of used to flying first class. Once you try it, it's kind of hard to go back to economy."

"I bet," I said. "Are you going to continue your nap on the plane?"

"Nah, I'm good. Plus, it's not that long of a flight. I'm all yours," he said.

I started getting that fluttery feeling in my stomach again. *No. Stop it.* I told myself. As we settled into our seats, I tried to get Aiden to tell me what his secret Madrid surprise was, but he wouldn't let the cat out of the bag.

"You'll just have to wait and see," he said. "Trust me, it's something you're going to like. Something you've been wanting to do for a long time."

Aiden knew that I didn't like surprises. I was a planner through and through. I was going to have to trust him, though. Right now, he seemed to know me better than anyone else.

As the plane landed, we took a cab to the hotel, which was gorgeously decorated and nestled right in the heart of Madrid. Just as I settled into my room, Aiden knocked at the door. "Are you ready?" he asked.

"Ready for what?" I replied.

"Ready for your surprise!" he smirked at me. "You're really going to like it."

"Hmmmm…I suppose," I replied, hesitantly. "You're not going to give me any hints or anything?"

"Nope," he said. "Just come with me and everything will be alright. I promise." He held out his hand to me and led me out the door and down to the lobby of the hotel. He hailed a cab for us, and the cab seemed to take us to a very shady part of Madrid.

"Are you taking me somewhere to murder me?" I asked him.

Aiden laughed. "No. Don't be fooled by the neighborhood. It's all part of the experience."

As we stepped out of the cab, I noticed a small building with a faded sign that said something about dancing. My Spanish was a little rusty, but I did know that much.

"Does that sign say something about dancing?" I asked him.

"Yes, it does. I know you've always wanted to take dancing classes, so here we are," Aiden said.

"What? Really?" I asked him, shocked. "We had to come all the way to Spain to take dancing classes?"

"Well, who knows better how to Flamenco than the Spanish?" Aiden asked.

"I suppose you're right about that," I said.

As we walked in, we were greeted by some very fancy-looking dance teachers who looked as if they had just performed at some international dance competition. They introduced themselves and handed me a giant, red, flowy skirt that they asked me to put on in the dressing room.

After I dressed, our dance teachers directed us to the middle of the floor to learn the basics of Flamenco dancing. I loved learning all the intricate moves with their stomps and skirt twirls. Aiden experienced some issues getting the footwork right and making the serious, angry faces they told him to make, but it all just made me laugh. I couldn't remember the last time I had had so much fun.

After learning the entire dance to the song we were listening to, our teachers asked if they could teach us another style of dance.

"What are they saying?" I asked Aiden. "My Spanish is'ot as great as it used to be."

"I think they said something about another dance," said Aiden. "I'm not sure, but it looks like they want to show us some different moves. Something other than Flamenco."

"Do they teach other styles too?" I asked.

"When I looked them up, it said they did all kinds of different dances from all over the world," Aiden said.

"Why do they want to teach us something different?" I asked.

"I'm not sure. Maybe they just think we'll be good at it," Aiden said.

"Okay," I replied, a little unsure.

The teachers motioned for me to remove the giant skirt and then told us to stand back in the middle of the floor. Then they showed us how to stand very close together and told us they were going to teach us how to dance the Rumba. At least that was what I got out of what they said. They immediately started teaching us how to move our hips along with the beat and do some body rolls. As if I wasn't laughing hard enough at Aiden attempting to get the footwork right in Flamenco, I laughed even harder as he looked even more confused and agitated at trying to move his hips and get the body rolls correct.

After the basic moves, though, the teachers put us even closer together and told Aiden to move his hand all the way up my body, starting at my ankle and going all the way up to the side of my face.

"Whoa, I don't know about that," I told him.

"Don't worry, Shelby. They are professionals. It's all in the name of dance!" he said as he gave a humorous little flourish.

I couldn't help but laugh at the silliness of it all. We stood right by each other, and I could feel the heat of his breath on the backside of my neck. They motioned for him to twirl me around and then move his hand slowly and seductively from the bottom to the top. I felt a shiver rise quickly up my spine. Suddenly, things weren't so funny anymore. I became acutely aware that Aiden was now touching my entire body. I turned my head back and noticed that it wasn't so funny for him anymore, either. As we locked eyes, our teachers started clapping.

"Whew! Caliente!" said Ernesto, the male teacher.

Aiden and I unhooked our bodies as quickly as possible and struggled to gather our composure. Maybe dancing a sensual dance like the Rumba was'ot such a good idea.

We thanked our teachers for the lesson and got in the cab to head back to the hotel to get ready before our soundchecks at the next venue.

"Well, what did you think?" Aiden asked.

"It was definitely...interesting," I replied.

"Yes. Interesting," Aiden agreed.

After that, we didn't say another word to each other until we got back to the hotel.

"So... soundcheck at 2?" I asked him.

"Yes. 2 o'clock sharp," he replied. "See you then."

It seemed neither one of us had the words to say to describe the experience we had just had. We hadn't touched each other like that in such a long time that it was both thrilling and a little bit alarming. I didn't really know what to think about it. The most alarming part of all of it, though, was how much I wanted to do it again.

Chapter Seventeen

When the cab arrived to take me to the soundcheck, I could hardly believe my eyes. This venue was even bigger than the one in London. I looked up to see an enormous metal and glass structure that looked like it could hold 100,000 people. *Surely, this can't be the right place,* I thought.

"Sir, is this the correct place?" I asked the driver. He seemed to only half understand what I was saying, but still responded, "Si, es correcto."

As I walked in and looked around, I started getting a little dizzy. I hoped that it would be the same kind of situation as the last venue where I could only see the first three rows of people, but in this place, there were seats all the way around the stage, so I wasn't sure it would work the same way.'

I headed toward the backstage area and found Aiden. "Aiden, how exactly is this going to work with the stage in the middle? This place is humongous!" I said.

"I know. It is pretty huge," he said. "Basically, there will be a pathway from here to the stage and you will have to walk through the crowd to get to the stage. I'll have some security guards surrounding me on my entrance, so if you want, you can use them as well."

"I'm not so worried about the security of it," I said. "I'm more concerned about freaking out after walking through all of those people and realizing just how many people are here."

"I wouldn't worry too much about that," Aiden said. "There are so many lights and special effects at this place that you won't be able to see a thing. You'll be lucky if you can even see Greg in this place."

Hearing this explanation made me feel a little better, but somehow, I doubted that he was right about that. "How am I going to focus on you instead of the crowd if you are in a totally different area of the building?" I asked him.

"Ah, I didn't think about that one," he said. "We'll have to get something else worked out. I'll give it some thought and let you know."

"Don't worry about it," I told him. "I can probably try to convince myself not to freak out on my own." I don't think I even convinced myself with that argument.

"No, no, no. I told you I'll be there for you, and I will find a way to be there for you," said Aiden.

We continued with the soundcheck, and I couldn't believe the kind of acoustics this venue had. Just little old me and an acoustic guitar echoed off the walls and sounded like an entire band from my spot on the stage. I didn't feel half as nervous as I thought I would in the middle of that gigantic place, but something told me it would be a totally different story that night at the performance.

After Aiden finished his soundcheck, he told me that he had a great idea. "Why don't we go to this bar around the corner and have a couple of sangrias before the show?" he asked. "It might help loosen you up and put you a little more at ease."

"Actually, that sounds like a good idea," I said. "I could use a good, stiff drink, and I do love me some sangria."

We headed out to the bar around the corner, which looked like the hippest place I had ever been in my life. Apparently, they were famous for numerous types of sangria, all of which were delicious, and all of which were super-high in alcohol content. Aiden was the responsible one and only had one, but silly me thought it would be a good idea to go ahead and try all of the flavors. I mean, how often do you get to sit in a hip bar and sip numerous types of sangria in actual Spain?

We arrived back at the venue just shy of 30 minutes to show-time, so I had barely any time to get myself ready. My head seemed to be spinning the entire time, so it is possible I put eyeliner on my lips and lip liner on my eyes, but I was feeling pretty good, so I really didn't care. The only thing I cared about was the fact that I was playing my songs in the biggest venue I'd ever been in, and I wasn't nervous at all. In fact, I was the most confident I had ever been before going out on stage!

A few moments later, it was showtime, and I was extremely lucky that Aiden had loaned me his security guards, or else I might not have found my way to the stage. I sat myself down on my stool and yelled out to everyone, "Okay, Spain! Are you ready to rock?" I wasn't even sure where that came from since I was about to play for them mostly slow acoustic ballads.

The show started out just fine, and I seemed to remember all of my lyrics to all of my songs (for the most part), but by the time I reached the fourth song, the entire room started to spin. I thought for a minute that I was going to blackout again like I had in London, but it turns out that fate had a different plan in mind. Just as I was in the middle of announcing what my next song was, I projectile vomited all of my delicious sangria and fruit all over the stage. I was completely mortified, and even more mortified that the entire concert had to come to a standstill while the poor concert venue workers climbed on stage to clean up my vomit.

By the time I got back on stage to finish my set, the audience had had about enough of me. I knew the show must go on, but I didn't think anyone was going to want to listen to me after the spectacle I had just presented to them. I looked all around the room and noticed that the lights were no longer blocking out all of the faces. All I could see around me were masses of angry Spanish Aiden fan faces until I arrived at the front row just to the right of the stage.

There was a man sitting at the edge of the row who was wearing a baseball cap, sunglasses, and a t-shirt that said "#1 Shelby fan." As I stared at this man questioningly, he pulled down his glasses to give me a little wink, and I realized that it was Aiden incognito. Seeing him gave me a little chuckle at my own expense, and I was able to go on with the next song. I decided it was probably about time to pick up the pace a little bit, so I played one of my more up-tempo songs, and that seemed to get the audience back on my side. I even busted a little bit out of my comfort zone and decided to get the audience on their feet and clap along to one of my songs. As I looked back at Aiden, he had the biggest smile on my face and seemed relieved that I had redeemed myself. He snuck backstage just before my last song to get ready for his own performance, but I already felt the immediate relief that his presence had given me. In the end, I felt like it wasn't an entirely failed performance, but I knew that Aiden was going to bring the house down the same way he always did.

I tried to sneak out a few times to try to catch some of Aiden's performance, but the crowd was so rowdy that it was a hopeless endeavor. I was able to see most of it on the giant screens that hung on both sides of the stage, though. I couldn't believe how incredibly popular Aiden was in other countries where the fans probably had no idea what he was even singing about. That was the way music worked, though. It was a universal language that crossed over all boundaries. It didn't always matter if you understood the message that was being presented. All that mattered was that you enjoyed the sounds being presented to you.

After his performance, Aiden came back to my dressing room, where I was trying my best to fend off the foreboding hangover lurking behind my eyes. "Hey, Shelby," he said as he walked in. "That was quite a show you put on out there." He gave me a wink and a smile.

"Well, I'm glad that at least my number one fan was there to witness the most embarrassing moment of my entire life," I replied.

"Yeah, I saw that guy. I had no idea you had your own merchandising people that sold shirts. I guess I need to step up my game," he said.

"Ugh, can we just forget this night even happened?" I asked him.

"Why would you want to do that?" Aiden asked. "Even though it seems terrible right now, this is going to make a great story someday. When we are old and gray, we'll look back at this moment as one of our crazy touring day disasters." Aiden immediately seemed to catch what he had just let slip out of his mouth and started to falter. "I mean, assuming we are still friends that far into the future."

I tried my best to help him save face. "I'm sure we will still be in touch with each other when we are old and gray," I said to try to help reassure him.

"Well, uh, I guess I will let you go and get some rest. I am assuming a post-concert nightcap is out of the question?" Aiden asked.

"Don't even mention the word 'alcohol' to me right now," I muttered. "I think I drank all of the wine in Spain, and now it is all over the stage."

"Yeah, I think I have a piece of pineapple stuck to the bottom of my shoe," Aiden teased.

"Gross. I really hope you're joking," I said turning beet red.

Aiden laughed. "Of course, I'm joking. Do you think I would really tell you if I did get a piece of fruit stuck under my shoe?" I threw a pillow at him. "I'll let you get back to nursing your soon-to-be hangover, then. Just don't forget that we have another early flight tomorrow morning to Rome."

"Ugh. I guess I'll be the one in sunglasses napping on the way to the airport this time, huh?" I asked.

"I suppose so," said Aiden. "Serves you right for making fun of me. I just hope you can make the same miraculous recovery I did." He smiled at me and told me goodnight.

When I got to the hotel, I didn't even bother to take a shower or peel off my clothes before plopping down on the bed and immediately falling asleep. I would experience all the after-effects the following morning, but when I stopped to look back on the day, I couldn't remember a time that I had had more fun in my life.

Chapter Eighteen

The early morning flight to Rome came much earlier than I was ready for, but I was happy that I had Aiden to help guide me through the hotel and airport. I vowed to myself never to drink Sangria again (at least not as much as I had in Spain) and tried to prepare myself mentally for the next concert.

I had always wanted to travel to Italy. I loved the food, the culture, and all the history that went along with Rome. I was hopeful that we would have some time to explore some of the magnificent tourist attractions and beautiful landmarks that Rome had to offer.

"Do you think we'll have much time to explore Rome?" I asked Aiden once we were settled into our seats.

"I sure hope so," he replied. "Italy is one of my favorite countries to travel to. Just wait until you try the coffee and all the amazing food. The wine is just to die for."

"Ugh, I don't think I'm ready to even hear the word 'wine' yet," I told him.

Aiden laughed. "You say that now, but once you try this wine, you'll think differently."

"What time do we have to be at the venue for soundcheck?" I asked him.

"I think around 3:00, which gives us plenty of time to explore and enjoy a nice, leisurely Italian lunch," he said.

"Just no more middle-of-the-day happy hours for me," I said.

"Deal," Aiden told me. "I'll do a better job of keeping an eye on you this time."

As our plane approached the great historical city of Rome, I was amazed at all of the ancient buildings I could pick out even from the sky. "Wow," I exclaimed. "I can't believe how beautiful it is, even from up here."

"I know," said Aiden. "I've been here so many times, but it never ceases to amaze me. All that history and beautiful architecture are just awesome to see in real life. Pictures really don't do it justice."

"I can't wait!" I said. I grabbed Aiden's hand in excitement as we started to descend. It wasn't a conscious action. Something about the excitement of being in a city I've always wanted to visit caused my body to have this involuntary reaction. "I'm sorry," I told him. "I don't know why I did that."

"That's okay," he said. "You were just caught up in the moment and excitement. It's perfectly okay to grab the hand of your close friend." He smiled at me.

The second we stepped out of the airport, I felt immersed in beauty and wonder. We hitched a cab and got settled into our hotel room, but I could hardly contain my excitement. Our hotel was nestled in the center of Rome, within walking distance to most of the major landmarks of the city. As soon as I had my luggage securely in my room, I immediately went to find Aiden's room and grab him for some city exploring.

I knocked enthusiastically on his door begging him to get going. "Okay, okay," he said. "I'm coming. Geez, relax, will ya? You'll get to see it all, don't worry. I have a plan for where we can go. I'll show you some of my favorite places to visit while I'm here."

"Yes! Let's go!" I said. We headed out and started with the Pantheon and Spanish steps before moving on to the Trevi Fountain. I was so entranced by the Trevi Fountain that I begged Aiden to come back at night so we could see it all lit up in its full glory. After all that walking, we decided to stop and get a bite to eat at a nearby cafe. I enjoyed a delicious Italian bread sandwich with prosciutto and fresh mozzarella. Aiden begged me to try one of their cappuccinos, and I was more than happy to oblige. If Heaven had a taste, I was sure that this would be it. All the flavors combined in such a fantastic way that I felt like I was tasting everything for the first time ever. I couldn't believe that just a sandwich and coffee could be so sublime.

We continued our walking tour of Rome with the Colosseum, the Roman Forum, and Palatine. I couldn't believe that so much history could be condensed into such a small part of the city. Then we visited an art museum near the Roman Forum, and I was so inspired by the amazing works of art that I decided to sit and write a song about them. I found a nearby bench and sat down with my notebook and pencil. When I looked up, I saw Aiden standing and staring at a large painting. I tried to take in all the artwork around me for inspiration, but for some reason, my eye kept returning to Aiden.

Aiden had such an easygoing way about him and a quiet confidence that I really admired. He wasn't ashamed to be who he really was. He had the attitude that you could either like him or not, he really didn't care either way. He made no apologies for being himself. He also had no fear of putting all his feelings out there in a song. Maybe no one really understood exactly what (or who) the song was about, but it wasn't for them anyway. It was his own form of therapy.

He seemed to be taking in all the various shapes, colors, and lines captured in the painting and seemed mesmerized by it. I watched the way his eyes moved through every inch of the painting, remembering when his eyes used to take in every inch of me in the same way. I could tell he was deep in thought, and I wondered what was on his mind. He always had that sense of mystery about him like you never really knew exactly what he was thinking. That day he was being somewhat incognito in his appearance by wearing a beige beanie hat and jean jacket, but I could tell he still caught the eye of a few admiring women. I don't know if they were recognizing him for his fame, or if they were just taking in those sparkling blue eyes of his. He was oblivious to them either way.

I glanced down at my paper and noticed that I hadn't written at all about the art that was staring me in the face, but rather about Aiden and the lines and shapes that he was creating. I didn't understand how I could be surrounded by so many priceless works of art, but the only priceless work of art I cared about was the man who stood in front of me. I took in the sight of his tall, slender body and recognized his ability to find beauty in every little thing he saw. He could have just as easily been staring at a trash can as at a painting, and he would still find something beautiful about it. That was one of the reasons I had fallen in love with him so long ago. No matter how down about myself I got, or how incredibly ugly I felt, he had a way of making me feel beautiful. He always said how there is so much power and beauty in the ordinary, but to him I would always be extraordinary.

Before long, it was time to head back to the hotel and prepare for the soundcheck.

"What did you think of all the sites?" Aiden asked me.

"It was really amazing," I told him. "I had a fantastic day today. Thank you for taking me around to see everything. I really appreciate it."

We just sat there looking at each other for what felt like an eternity. It seemed that there wasn't any more that needed saying. We understood each other in a way that neither one of us even needed to speak.

Everything seemed to go smoothly at the soundcheck, and I was even more amazed at this venue than I was at the gigantic concert hall in Madrid. This one was much smaller and held much fewer people, but it was a grand, elaborate opera house that was the most beautifully decorated place I had ever been in.

As I was getting ready for the concert, I noticed I was taking even more care in my appearance tonight. There wasn't any clear-cut reason why, but deep down I knew exactly why. I was feeling better than I had in a long time. I was starting to feel like myself again, and I knew the person who was responsible for making me feel this way. I wanted to repay him somehow, but I couldn't think of any way that would be fitting. How do you pay someone back for bringing you back to life? I decided a nice dinner after the concert was a good start.

Before the concert, I pulled Greg aside and told him that I had an idea for a solo acoustic performance that I would like to do. I said that I was going to perform a cover song and dedicate it to Aiden and asked Greg to make sure Aiden was paying attention. I felt like I had one more "thank you" to offer him before taking him to dinner that night.

Towards the end of my set, I announced to the crowd that I had a special cover song I wanted to perform for a special friend. Greg exited the stage and made sure that Aiden had a clear view of me. Then I started to sing the song, "Because You Loved Me" by Celine Dion. The range was a little difficult for me, but I decided to switch it up and make the song my own. I slowed it down and emphasized certain parts that I knew Aiden would pay special attention to. I tried to focus my eyes on Aiden throughout the song so I could telepathically communicate a "thank you" to him. I knew somehow, he would understand exactly what I was saying. I could see him tearing up towards the end of the song.

Aiden of course was amazing during his set. He seemed to have renewed energy and vigor with every show. I couldn't understand how he could be like that when I felt like all my energy was drained with each show, and I was struggling just to make it through to the next city. I knew this was just the tip of the iceberg for him, and he was used to playing many more shows on a U.S. tour and traveling to a new city each night. I wasn't so sure I was cut out for the touring life and didn't know if my voice could take it, but Aiden seemed like he was born to be on the stage. He knew exactly how to take total command of the stage and somehow knew just what the audience wanted to hear next. He was able to put together an ebb and flow to a show that never left you feeling bored. I found myself wishing that I had half the talent he did.

After the concert, we headed out to a little bistro that was known for making the best pasta in Rome along with some live musical entertainment. One of the best things about Italy was that the restaurants stayed open late, which was great news for musicians on tour. We started our meal off with some burrata, fresh bread, bruschetta, and glasses of Chianti. Aiden opted for some spaghetti bolognese, and I went for a chicken and pesto pasta dish. They were both magnificent. Dessert was a delightfully creamy tiramisu and a glass of super-sweet Passito. As we were eating dessert, a man who was singing and playing the guitar came up to our table.

"Lei parla inglese?" he asked us.

"Si," we both told him.

"Beautiful couple!" he said to us before starting to sing a beautiful Italian love song. We continued sipping our wine and swaying along to his lovely song, but then he told us, "Beautiful couple, dance!"

Aiden and I both looked at each other and shrugged before standing up to slow dance together. It felt so natural to be in his arms, swaying along together to the music. I had forgotten the feeling of the touch of his hand against my back and the smell of his cologne. I just wanted to take a mental snapshot of that moment and remember it forever. I didn't know if I was getting tipsy from all the wine or was lost in the moment of slow dancing with a beautiful man in the heart of Rome, but the sensation was very seductive and addicting.

For a moment toward the end of the song, we both stopped and looked into each other's eyes. I knew there were feelings there for both of us, but we both knew they weren't feelings we could explore. We continued to stare at each other, almost daring each other to say out loud the words we both thought. We were taken out of our reverie by the guitarist saying to us, "Kiss! Kiss!"

Aiden and I pulled apart from each other, and I just told him, "No, no. Not a couple."

"Ah, mi scusi," said the guitarist as he bowed and continued to the next table.

Aiden and I both sat back down and took big gulps of our wine, neither of us really knowing what to say. We just looked around awkwardly sipping our wine, until finally, Aiden said, "Well, should we go?"

"Yes, please," I told him. "Any more of this wine and I won't be able to even walk back to the hotel."

We began the walk back to the hotel and noticed we could see the huge, bright moon just between all of the buildings. It was a near-perfect night. The sky was so clear that the stars seemed to be shining even brighter. The only thing lingering was the words that had been left unsaid by both of us.

"Listen, Shelby," Aiden said suddenly, as he stopped and took hold of my hand in the middle of the cobblestone walkway.

"What is it?" I asked him, feigning ignorance.

"I don't know about you, but these past few days have been bringing up some feelings that I thought were buried deep down inside," he said. "I know it's really not the right time for either of us, but I can feel myself starting to fall back in love with you."

I couldn't believe that he had actually had the guts to say it. He wasn't saying it through song. He wasn't just making me think he was saying it with his eyes. He was saying the actual words that I had secretly longed for him to say since that day I saw him again in Austin.

"Aiden, we can't," I said. "I can't do this. I can't do that to you and your wife. I can't put myself through those feelings with you again. I can't get my heart broken by you again. I just can't." I was starting to tear up, and he could see it.

"I'm not asking you to do anything," Aiden said. "I just thought I should finally say the thing I have been thinking for a very long time. I just wanted to get it out there, so it wouldn't be hanging over my head anymore. Please don't cry."

He placed his hand on the side of my cheek and started pulling my face toward his own. At that moment, I turned and ran down the walkway away from him. I didn't want to go down that path again. It didn't matter how comfortable and at ease he made me feel. It didn't matter how he made me feel like myself again after so many years of wondering if I was going to be lost to the world forever. It didn't matter that he still gave me the butterfly feeling in the pit of my stomach every time I laid eyes on him. It didn't matter that I had secretly been in love with him for 20 years. No matter how much my heart longed for him, my head was always going to win, so it just didn't matter.

Chapter Nineteen

The next morning, I woke in my gorgeous hotel in Rome, dreading seeing Aiden again after last night. I had been longing to kiss him for so long, and when the opportunity presented itself that night, I had surprised myself by resisting that urge. We were off to the next city, and I had no idea how I was going to face Aiden or what I was going to say to him.

I packed up my things and reluctantly headed down to the lobby to catch a taxi to the train station. Predictably, Aiden was there waiting for me. As I approached him, I decided the best thing to do was just to smile and pretend like nothing had happened.

"Good morning, Shelby," he said. "Ready to head off to Milan?"

"Sounds fantastic," I replied.

After that short exchange, we both stood there awkwardly waiting for the cab to arrive. Once we got in, Aiden of course had to break the silence.

"Listen, Shelby, about last night..." he said.

"Aiden, please..." I interrupted. "I really don't want to talk about it. Can we please just go to Milan and focus on the concert tonight?"

"Okay," Aiden replied. "If you don't want to talk about it, we don't have to. Just know that I don't regret telling you what I did."

We sat in silence for the remainder of the cab ride and for most of the train ride as well. We plugged in our respective headphones, both took out our notebooks, and just focused on doing our jobs. Before I knew it, on that short train ride to Milan, I had written a whole new song:

I hate that I love you.
No, it can't be true.
You have her,
And I have my dreams too.

We've tried to be friends.
We've tried something more.
But nothing will work,
We've been here before.

We should just go our separate ways.
You and I will see better days.

I hate that I love you.
No, it can't be true.
You're not the one I'm meant for,
And I'm not the one for you.

My heart has to be lying,
'Cause it's just too hard to bear.
I have to give up trying.

I hate that I love you.

I felt relieved to get my feelings out and on paper. Songwriting is such a therapy to me and singing my words out loud at the concert that night would be even more of a weight off my shoulders. I was sure Aiden was going to see right through me, but the less I said to him, the better. My plan was to try to avoid him as much as possible and pretend the previous night hadn't even happened.

My plan didn't work out as I would have liked because Aiden, of course, wanted to talk to me the second we arrived in Milan.

"Listen, Shebly," he said. "Can we just take a little walk after checking in and have a little chat? I think it would be good for us to talk things through."

I exhaled. "Fine. If that's what you want to do, that's fine," I replied.

We decided to take a walk and check out the Duomo, which was surrounded by hordes of tourists but was still beautiful. nonetheless. We found a bench near the cathedral so we could sit and face each other while having the conversation I dreaded.

"Shelby, I know you don't want to talk about this, but I don't want to go on ignoring each other for the rest of the tour," Aiden said. "I'm sorry about what I said last night. I realize now that I should have just kept my mouth shut, and we should have just continued on with how things are going. We have a good thing going with our friendship, and I'm sorry if I messed it up by trying to make it more."

I breathed a sigh of relief. "Thank you for saying that," I said. "I really don't want to mess up our friendship either. It has been so nice to spend time with you again and have someone around who really understands me and can understand how important my songwriting is to me."

"Of course," Aiden replied. "I feel the same way about you. We complement each other so nicely, and for some reason, I didn't see how much things would mess up between us if we tried to make it something more."

"Exactly," I said. "So can we go back to just being songwriting partners and tour mates and forget that whole conversation even happened?"

"Definitely," Aiden said. "Let's just enjoy Milan together as friends and have a great show tonight." Aiden checked his watch. "We better get going. We have an earlier-than-usual sound check."

We got up from the bench and grabbed a cab back to the hotel to get ready for soundcheck. I had decided to play my newly-written song at the concert that night, but I wasn't going to debut it at the soundcheck. I felt confident that it would sound better on the fly and in the moment. It would be an intimate, acoustic guitar only performance, and I didn't need to test it out with my backup guitarist or the sound system.

After the soundcheck, I headed back to the hotel to get dressed and prepare myself for what I knew would be a very raw and vulnerable performance. I wasn't sure if it was a good thing or not that most people didn't even know who I was, and even if they did, most of them didn't speak English. They weren't there to see me anyway. They were there for Aiden. Being armed with that knowledge was freeing in a way. I could pretty much sing whatever I wanted to and get some practice on some songs I wasn't so sure about. The only thing I was nervous about was debuting my new song to Aiden. I knew he was going to see right through me.

I heard a knock on the door and went to answer it. There, in front of the door, was a dozen red roses (my favorite), with a card that simply said. "Looking forward to a great concert tonight, friend." Just thinking about Aiden's thoughtfulness made me smile. Even though it was a historically romantic gesture, Aiden knew that I didn't really like getting flowers because I was bound to kill those flowers in about five minutes. I put a few last-minute touches on my appearance and then headed down to the concert hall.

As I prepared to take the stage, Aiden came up behind me and said, "I just want to apologize again. I know I made things awkward between us, and that is the last thing I want. I have really been enjoying spending this time with you."

"It's no problem, really," I responded. "Have a great show."

"You, too. Break a leg," he said.

I took the stage and started with my well-rehearsed and well-known songs (at least to me), but then took a deep breath and prepared myself to sing my new song.

"I actually just wrote this song today, so I would like you all to enjoy the world debut," I said to the crowd. "I hope you like it."

I took a seat on the stool as my backup guitarist made his exit to allow for a more intimate feel. The spotlight shone directly on me as I began to sing my new song. I focused solely on the words and playing the guitar. I knew the second I glanced over to Aiden, I would experience those unwelcome feelings again.

By the time I finished, I casually glanced over to behind the curtains to see Aiden with a confused look on his face. He gave me one last glance and then walked away. I wasn't sure how to interpret that glance. The thought made me confused myself, but I knew I had to continue and finish my set.

After the concert, I tried to find Aiden to talk, but he was nowhere to be found. I didn't know if he decided to hang out with some other friends or went straight to the hotel. I decided it was best just to head to the hotel myself so I could prepare myself for the next day's concert in Paris.

Paris was a city I was beyond excited to visit. I had always wanted to go there, so I wanted to look over my schedule for the day and make sure I could get in plenty of sightseeing before the soundcheck. I knew we would be taking a plane for this one, so I also wanted to make sure I could gather all my things in plenty of time to make it to the airport.

I wasn't sure what my morning would look like and if Aiden would want to talk to me or not, but I did know I didn't even want to think about it. I had my career to think about, and I needed to focus on that. Aiden would always be on the back of my mind just like he had been for all of those years I was without him, so it was no good thinking about him right now. I knew I had to try to get some sleep, but I also knew it wasn't going to happen. I was in for a long night of overanalyzing my emotions about Aiden, yet again.

Chapter Twenty

The alarm clock rang before I was really prepared to get the day started, but my excitement for Paris made up for the lack of sleep. All night long, my brain tried to interpret every glance, every gesture, and every word Aiden had said to me in the past few days. I tried to force my mind to stop and get some sleep, but it was no use.

I gathered my things and headed down to the hotel lobby, where a car waited to take me to the airport. Aiden was nowhere in sight. I asked the driver if he was going to take Aiden to the airport as well, and he told me that Aiden had opted to take an earlier flight and was already well on his way.

That's strange, I thought. *Why would Aiden completely change his plans and not even bother to tell me?*

I immediately pushed the thought out of my mind and focused on my excitement for the day ahead. I had spent enough time trying to analyze Aiden's every move and thought. I was now headed to a city I had always wanted to travel to, and I was going to make the most of it. I had already picked out my perfect Parisian outfit for the day, planned on taking a nice morning walk along the Seine River and having a decadent latte at a quaint cafe along the river.

As soon as I stepped out of the airport, I took in the sights and sounds of Paris. It was exactly as I had imagined. Although it was not a particularly sunny or warm day, the clouds and cool, damp weather seemed to add to the mysterious quality Paris had to offer. I hailed a cab to the hotel and checked in quickly to make sure I had enough time for plenty of exploration. I put on my striped short-sleeved shirt, black skirt, and black ballet flats and began to explore the city doing my best impression of a Parisian girl who belonged there, even though I'm sure I stuck out as a tourist like a sore thumb.

As I walked along the river, I found the perfect little cafe and ordered a croissant and latte before sitting down outside and enjoying some people watching on one of the most beautiful streets in the city. It was a bit chilly and overcast, so the street wasn't as busy as I'm sure it usually is. I pondered my setlist for that night and questioned which songs would go best with my Parisian setting, when a familiar face started strolling my way, camera in hand.

"Shelby, hey," Aiden said as he came up next to me, sounding more awkward than usual.

"Hi, Aiden" I responded. "I didn't know you were planning on taking an earlier flight and getting here sooner than me." I tried to hide the accusation in my voice, but I was a little annoyed that he hadn't even bothered to let me know his plans beforehand.

"Yeah, I wanted to get a little sightseeing in, and I knew it was going to be a busy day for me, so I came a little early," he said as if there was absolutely nothing wrong with what he had done.

"It would have been nice to have a heads up about your plans," I said.

"I'm sorry about that," he replied, head hanging down. "I just had a lot on my mind and wasn't really considering proper social protocol."

"That's okay. I just wasn't sure if it was something I said or did to upset you," I said.

"No, you didn't do anything wrong," Aiden answered. "I just had some thinking to do."

"I see," I said, a bit skeptical. "Well, you're welcome to join me if you'd like."

"Sure thing. I'll just place my order and I'll be right out," he said.

Aiden went into the cafe and ordered an espresso and then joined me at the outside table. He snapped a few pictures before settling in.

"Do you always take a lot of pictures when you are traveling?" I asked.

"Yeah, it's kind of become a hobby of mine," he said. "I like to capture little things about a place that not many people notice. There's a lot of beauty in the ordinary."

"I suppose that's true," I told him. "You have such a good eye for those kinds of things. I can't even work my phone camera properly. I probably couldn't even take a good selfie."

Aiden laughed. "You just need the proper equipment. There have been great advances in phone technology, but nothing can quite replace a good high-quality point-and-click. Check out all the features on this one." He leaned in to show me all the different buttons and switches on his camera. "I particularly like the older versions better because you get a more pure shot without over-the-top extras." He took a picture of me.

"Uh, you could at least warn a girl!" I laughed at him.

"Sorry. It was good lighting and a beautiful subject," he smiled at me.

"Or, just the ordinary again," I told him.

"No, this one is definitely extraordinary," he said.

I blushed immediately and decided to change the subject. "So, tell me about where we're playing tonight."

Just as Aiden was about to answer, the sky opened up and rain came pouring down on us in heavy sheets. Neither Aiden nor I had umbrellas with us, so we ran as fast as we could to the nearest cover, which was under a bridge on the sidewalk. As soon as we were under the bridge, Aiden gave me a very serious and concerned look.

"Shelby, I have to ask. Who is your latest song about?" Aiden asked.

"What do you mean?" I asked him, even though I knew exactly what he was getting at.

"I think you know what I mean," he answered. "I heard all the lyrics. Don't think I can't still see you through your songwriting."

I looked into his sparkling blue eyes for what felt like forever before deciding to answer. "It's about you. Of course, it is. They are all about you."

Aiden immediately grabbed my face in his hands and leaned in for the most passionate kiss I had ever experiencedin my life. Even with the commotion, rainstorm, and people all around us, all I could focus on was him and that moment. It was as if our bodies were finally reacting and giving in to the emotions that had been running through us since that day in Austin. After all that time we had spent in close quarters pretending that we could just be friends, it was a sweet release. I sunk deeper into the kiss and never wanted it to end. Aiden had always been a good kisser, but this was something much more. This was the physical manifestation of years of desire and longing.

After what felt like hours, the rain finally let up, and we pulled away from our kiss. A street performer I hadn't noticed before came out from under the bridge on the opposite side and began playing "Le Vie En Rose" on his violin. I felt like I was living in a dream. We just stood there, staring at each other for the longest time, when my head immediately started telling me, *Run!* This time I ignored the voice in my head and instead listened to my heart.

"How long do we have before soundcheck?" I asked Aiden.

"We have a while. About four hours or so," he replied.

"Good," I smiled at him. "Come with me."

We took a cab back to the hotel and very discreetly made our way up to my room. It was all happening in such a hurry, that I didn't even have time to think. I was done thinking things through first. I just wanted to finally act on what I had been craving for so long. The moment the door clicked into place, our lips were interlocked again. We seemed to move in slow motion toward the bed and fell into a natural rhythm with each other. Even though it had been many years since we'd been intimate with each other, everything felt natural and easy between us. I didn't know if it was because of our familiarity with each other, our similarities, or if it was just because our bodies had been craving each other for so long, but those four hours passed before we even realized it.

By the time I finally checked the clock, I said, "Geez, Aiden. We need to get going! It's almost time for soundcheck already. We didn't even eat lunch!"

"Well, I don't know about you, but my appetite was certainly satisfied," Aiden said as he smiled at me.

"Mmmm, me too," I said kissing his lips one last time before rolling out of bed. "We do need to re-enter the world at some point, though."

"I'll just try to sneak out over to my room and allow you some time to get dressed," Aiden said. "Shelby?"

"Yes?" I replied.

"That was magical," he said. "I feel like I've been keeping all of that bottled up inside for so long, and it was a great release."

"Me too," I said, smiling at him. "I'll see you at soundcheck."

As soon as he closed the door behind him, I collapsed back onto the bed. *What the hell was I thinking? What did I just do?* Immediately a sense of dread filled my head, but my body was so delightfully satisfied and happy at the moment that I didn't want to even consider the consequences of my actions.

Pull it together, Shelby, I thought. *You have a show to put on tonight. No more daydreaming about how amazing Aiden is.*

I finally pulled myself out of bed and got ready to head down to soundcheck. Aiden and I took a cab together, and I couldn't stop looking at him or smiling. He seemed to have me under a captivating spell. Every time he looked over at me with that twinkle in his eyes, I got butterflies in my stomach all over again.

For the entire soundcheck, whenever he or I practiced one of our love songs, we made a point to look over to the other one and smile. It was like we were in our own special world that no one else could permeate. I was floating on air and didn't feel like coming down any time soon.

After the soundcheck, we headed back to the hotel and decided to go to his room and order some room service. We hadn't had a sip of alcohol, but we were both drunk on being with each other. I instructed Aiden to sit on the bed and began playing "Something He Can Feel" by Aretha Franklin on my phone.

"Wow, I really need to change clothes for tonight's show," I said to him seductively as I started to undress.

"Yeah, you do," he said. "I guess you better change out of those dirty clothes." He gave me a knowing smile.

As I slowly removed my clothes, I danced around the room to the song and came closer to him, ready to tear off every inch of his clothing. I peeled off his tight t-shirt to reveal his round shoulders and chest hair before running my hands up and down his chest and then pushing him down onto the bed. My body couldn't get enough of his, and I felt purely carnal.

We surrendered ourselves to each other and came up for air whenever we needed it, but mostly our bodies made up for all of that lost time. There was so much pent-up sexual energy between us that

I wasn't sure we'd ever be able to stop. Eventually, it really was time to start getting ready for the show, so I had to find a way to sneak my way out of his room and make it over to my own.

I tried my best to concentrate as I was getting ready, but I was so high on Aiden and couldn't seem to get enough. Lost in my daydream, I heard a knock on the door. A smile crept across my face as I went to answer it, expecting to find Aiden on the other side.

"Did you…" I started saying as I opened the door, but my jaw dropped immediately when I saw who was on the other side.

Chapter Twenty-One

"Did I what? Were you expecting someone?" Chris said through the large bouquet of flowers he held in his hands.

"Oh, nothing," I replied, still in shock. "I was just expecting them to bring me some more towels."

"I guess you'll be needing a few more now that you have an unexpected visitor," Chris said smiling slyly at me and walking through the door.

"Chris, what are you doing here?" I asked him.

"I have a few days off from work and saw that your tour was taking you through Paris, so I thought, 'What better use of my time than to fly to the most romantic city on earth and spend some time with the most beautiful woman on earth?'" he asked.

"Wow. I don't really know what to say," I told him. "I can't believe you flew all the way here just to see me."

"I didn't want to miss the chance to see you on your first big tour and maybe get a chance to explore the city with you a bit," he said.

"The show is actually really soon, so there's not a whole lot of time for sightseeing," I told him.

"Well, the only sight I really wanted to see is the one in front of me right now," he came in closer to me and began kissing me slowly on the neck.

"Chris, I'm really flattered, but I literally have zero time right now," I told him, flustered and not really sure what to say.

"Ah, gotcha," he replied, obviously a little upset. "Well, we wouldn't want to rush a good thing anyway, now would we?" He smiled at me. "Let's head down to your show! I can't wait to hear you."

"Great! You can just ride along with me and hang backstage if you'd like," I told him.

As we arrived at the concert venue, the wheels were turning in my mind, trying to figure out what I was going to say to Aiden, what I was going to say to Chris, and how on earth I was going to get myself out of this mess.

"So, are you excited to be playing in Paris?" Chris asked me.

"Yes, of course," I told him. "I've always wanted to travel here. I took a walk this morning along the river and was able to sample some delicious French cuisine." I tried to make it sound as if I had spent my day jet setting all around Paris rather than just exploring the beautiful landscape that is Aiden's body.

"Sounds like you had a good time," Chris said. "I hope I can make your night even more enjoyable." He flashed me that million megawatt smile of his and looked straight at me with those piercing blue eyes. There was no way I was going to be able to turn him down. Here was the most gorgeous man in front of me, offering himself to me (though I still couldn't understand why), and all I could think about was Aiden.

I just smiled back at him and tried to focus on the show ahead of me. Just as I had feared, I spotted Aiden backstage, and he smiled at me and began making his way over. He hadn't noticed Chris at first, but as soon as it dawned on him that Chris was there, his smile faded quickly from his face.

"Hey, Aiden!" Chris said as Aiden approached.

"Hey Chris," Aiden replied, a little taken aback. "How's it going? You decided to make a little impromptu trip to Paris, huh?"

"I couldn't resist seeing this amazing woman do what she does best," Chris said. "And in one of the most beautiful cities on the planet? Nothing better."

"Well, no one can blame you for that," Aiden said, looking back at me questioningly.

"Yes, he definitely surprised me at my hotel room door today," I said, trying to telepathically apologize to Aiden while I said it.

Just as things were starting to get even more awkward, the stage manager came up to me and said it was almost time to start.

"I guess I better get going," I said. I took a deep breath and began to head out to the stage. As I glanced back, I saw both Aiden and Chris standing there watching me take the stage. I felt much more nervous about the love triangle situation that was forming than I did about the gigantic crowd in front of me. I tried to gather my courage and play my setlist just like I had in the other shows, but my heart was definitely not in it that night. My head spun in a million different directions, and I really wasn't sure what I should do. The whole day had felt like a big whirlwind of emotions, most of which were good up until that moment.

The entire day with Aiden had been the most amazing day I had in a very long time, if not in my entire life. We had a spark between us that was undeniable and understood each other on a level that I had never experienced with anyone else before. We were connected to each other not just as two people who were attracted to each other, but our souls seemed to be tethered together as well. It was not just a physical attraction. He was the most humble, selfless, caring, and passionate man that I had ever met in my life. We had such a deep understanding of each other that we didn't even need to communicate what the other one was thinking. It was like we just knew.

Aiden had his faults, too. He could be impulsive, overly emotional, sometimes stubborn, and obviously, being married was a big hindrance to our situation as well.

Chris arriving on the scene made a complicated situation nearly impossible. I genuinely thought that Chris thought of me just as a fling. I certainly thought of him that way. Still, I was touched that he thought of me and had flown all this way to support me and spend time with me. No one had ever made such a bold move on my behalf before.

Chris was a much simpler choice and was so much fun to be around. I also couldn't stop staring at him. The man was a Greek god. It's not often you find a man who is so unbelievably gorgeous, but also funny, kind, and smart. He had a lot going for him. The choice should be an easy one. Looking back at all the facts and thinking logically about my situation, there was no doubt about what I should do. I knew what I had to do, but I had to act quickly before any more mistakes were made.

Chapter Twenty-Two

Once the concert was over, I found no sign of Aiden anywhere. I had some important things to talk to him about, but apparently, he was wanting nothing to do with me at that point. I decided it was best to just head back to my hotel room alone, and maybe I could find Aiden there and have a chat.

I had just had a hard conversation with Chris about how I had discovered some long-buried feelings for Aiden while we were touring. He told me that he understood and could tell that I still had feelings for him when we were back in Los Angeles. He was visibly upset, but I think he didn't have a shortage of his choice of women back home in L.A. I couldn't believe that I had just let a man like that go. How often do you find a man that is so seemingly perfect on both the outside and the inside? I was not looking for perfect, though. I was looking for my person. In my mind and heart, there was always only one person for me, and that man's name was Aiden. I had to find him and tell him right away.

I reached my hotel room and decided to freshen up a bit and order a bottle of champagne from room service to try to smooth things over with Aiden. I took a deep breath, headed down the hallway, and knocked on the door, hoping Aiden would feel the same way I did.

To my surprise, the door was answered by Natasha. "Shelby, hi!" she said. She leaned in and gave me a hug. "What's the champagne for? Did you hear the news already? I guess news travels fast!"

"Oh, um…" I started, not sure what to say. "Of course! Congratulations!" I wasn't sure if that was the correct response, but I was hoping the news was good news, at least for her.

"Aiden, Shelby is here with some champagne for you, since obviously, I can't have any!" Natasha yelled across the room.

Aiden came to the door with a look of shock on his face. I could tell that he was still processing the news himself. "Hey, Shelby," he said. "How did you know? Did you know about this before I did or something?"

"Um, Aiden, could you come out into the hallway for a quick second?" I asked him.

"Sure thing," he said.

As soon as he was in the hallway, I had to find out what was happening.

"Aiden, what the hell is going on? Why is Natasha here?" I asked him.

"So, you can have surprise visitors, but I can't? Is that why Chris came out here to see you? Did you already know about this?" Aiden sounded very accusing.

"I don't even know what you are talking about, and I had no idea that Chris was planning on coming out here," I said. "I just ended things with him, and he is on the next flight home."

"Wait, what? You ended things with Chris?" he asked.

"Yes," I took a deep breath. "I told him I was in love with someone else."

Before Aiden could respond, Natasha popped her head out into the hallway with a striped Parisian onesie. "Aiden, just look at this!

Won't it be so cute for the baby? It could be for either a boy or a girl! This is so exciting!" she said.

"Uh, yeah, Natasha. That looks great," Aiden said. "Just give us one more minute and I'll be right back in."

Natasha retreated into the room, and I slowly turned to look at Aiden. "So, she's pregnant?"

"Apparently so," Aiden said. "She just found out and flew out to tell me the news. She's going to come along for the rest of the tour also, so I can help take care of her."

"I see," I responded, looking down at the floor.

"Look, Shelby, I'm not sure what to say. I had no idea that Natasha was pregnant. What happened with us yesterday…"

I stopped him right away. "Don't worry about it. I guess we both just lost control a bit. I don't know what we were thinking. Please, don't worry about me. Just go back in there with Natasha and celebrate your good news," I handed him the bottle of champagne. "Here, take this. Congratulations."

I turned to leave as quickly as I could. I could feel the tears welling up in my eyes and wanted to escape. I didn't know how I could have misread the situation so badly. I should have known that he didn't feel the same way I did. It must have been just a fluke. He was just getting it all out of his system before settling down with his real family and becoming a dad. I knew this wasn't something I was going to get over right away, but I needed to be by myself for a while and indulge in a good cry before figuring out my next move.

Chapter Twenty-Three

I didn't have much time to grieve my heartache because the next morning we were off to the next city. We were headed to Berlin. We only had two more cities to go in the European leg of the tour, so I needed to focus on my performance and not let any personal feelings or situations get in my way. I packed up and headed down to the lobby to check out and grab a cab to the airport for my flight.

I didn't bother to wait for Aiden because I didn't think I could face him after what had transpired the night before. I was still feeling a little stung from the breakup with Chris, and then Natasha dropped that big bombshell on me, which hurt even worse. In my head, I knew that what Aiden and I had done was wrong and of course, I realized that he was a married man and was not likely to leave his wife, but my emotions still got the best of me, and I had been holding out hope. All that hope was lost now. It didn't matter what I thought I felt or how "made for each other," I thought we were. He had made a commitment to his wife, and I needed to get out of the way. Just as the day before I had felt giddy and content, I now felt slimy and dirty. I was the other woman, a role that I never thought I would find myself in. I was always the good girl. What the hell was I thinking getting in the way of a marriage like that?

I hoped we could just forget about the whole thing and put it behind us. I knew it was going to prove to be somewhat difficult since we were still touring together, but I had to find a way to put my feelings aside. I would most likely just channel it into my songwriting, the way I had always done before. Don't some of the best songs come out of personal heartbreak anyway? Maybe some of my best songwriting would come from this.

I arrived at the airport and received my boarding pass, and by the time I headed to the gate, I saw Aiden and Natasha heading my way. Of course, they were on the same flight, so there was no way I could avoid them at this point. Once they were checked in, they came and sat down next to me and began to chat.

"Shelby, are you excited to go to Berlin? I've never been there before. I'm sure it's beautiful," Natasha said.

"Yes, I hear there are some really great places to visit there," I told her.

"I just hope I can keep up with everyone now that I am with child," Natasha said. "That morning sickness is starting to kick in, so I'm not sure how well I'll travel."

"Yeah, mine was pretty bad, but you'll get used to it," I said.

"That's right. You've had two kids, haven't you?" she asked me. "I have all kinds of questions to ask you! I don't know how you can leave those precious little darlings behind while you travel all over Europe, but I suppose to each his own! I'm going to grab some water and then pick your brain for a while."

I couldn't help but feel a little offended at Natasha's little dig at me. Was she really going to criticize my parenting abilities when she hasn't even had her own child yet? I decided to just blow past it and look up things I wanted to do in Berlin to distract me from my current situation.

As I opened my laptop, though, I could not keep my focus on all the wonderful Berlin attractions. My mind kept wandering to Aiden and my feelings for him. Rather than trying to avoid thinking about him, I decided to do what I always did: channel my feelings into a song.

Chorus:
I want you but I can't have you.
Why do you make me feel this way?
Tell me, what is it that I can do?
Tell me, what can I say?
When I want you, but I can't have you.

When you look into her eyes,
This feeling just comes over me,
That kind of look I just despise.
Why can't you just let me be?

Chorus

She doesn't know how lucky she has it.
She doesn't know how special you are.
I'd like to, but I just can't quit.
How could you let it come this far?

Chorus

Bridge:
Why can't you be hurtful and mean?
Why can't you be an average guy?
You're one of the greatest guys I've ever seen.
I want to stop, so tell me why.

Chorus

As soon as I finished typing the words, Aiden came up behind me. I immediately closed my laptop. I glanced up at him, face most likely beet red.

"What are you working on?" Aiden asked me.

"Just working on an idea for a new song," I answered him.

"Ah," he answered, seemingly knowing exactly what it was all about. "Listen, about Natasha…"

"Aiden, please," I told him. "You don't need to explain or justify anything. Really. We just made a mistake one night, and let's leave it at that."

"So, you think it was a mistake?" he asked me.

"Yes, of course, it was! You are a married man, and now you are having a baby! What part of what we did was not a mistake?" I asked him, incredulously.

"I know you're right," he sighed. "I just thought…" he started but was interrupted by Natasha.

"I swear, I feel like I can't get enough water right now! It's like this baby is severely dehydrated or something!" Natasha said, smiling. "What are you guys talking about?"

"Oh, nothing," I answered. "Aiden was just helping me out with my setlist for Berlin."

"Oh, good," Natasha said. "You know, Shelby, you might want to consider throwing in some newer, maybe faster songs. Something fresh might liven up the performance."

I glared at her. "Thanks for the tip," I said through gritted teeth.

"Oh, Aiden, won't it be so romantic, strolling around Berlin together?" Natasha asked Aiden.

"Um, yeah. Although, I don't know how much time I'll have for sightseeing. Right when we arrive. I have soundcheck, but we can maybe stroll around town a little bit after," Aiden answered.

"Just make sure to make time for your family!" Natasha said, rubbing her belly.

Before long, it was time to board our plane. I was thankful that I had a seat far enough away from Aiden and Natasha that I didn't have to think about the whole love triangle situation or listen to Natasha's excessive gushing over Aiden and their baby. I tried to find it within myself to be happy for them, but the jealous part of me took over and all I wanted was Aiden. I felt so selfish and foolish, but I just wanted that time with him back. I kept thinking to myself what would have happened if things had been different? What if I had gone with him in college instead of staying? I wouldn't have ended up with my two amazing children, but I also wouldn't have gone through a terrible marriage and ultimate divorce. I tried to shift my mind onto other things because I knew it would do no good to dwell on what might have been.

Chapter Twenty-Four

By the time we got to Berlin, things seemed much clearer to me. Why was I dwelling on something that was never going to happen? I need to let things go and focus on my new career. Here I was playing a major tour with one of the most sought-after musicians in the world, so why am I so focused on my feelings for Aiden? The sensible side of me started taking over and focusing on the day ahead. With only two cities left in the European leg of the tour, I had to get my head in the game and make sure I made as much of an impact as I could in the little time I had left in Europe.

As we touched down in Berlin, we all got settled into our hotel rooms, and soon it was time for sound check. As much as I hated to admit it, I thought that maybe my set could use a little refresh, as Natasha so astutely pointed out, so I decided to try out some newer songs. There was one in particular that I had never played live before, so I gave it a shot during sound check.

Why are you doing this to me?
I was happy before you came into my life.
I had no reason to leave.
How can something so wrong feel so right?

I was with somebody else,
And you had tons of other girls pleading by your side.
I have battled with myself,
But these feelings I just cannot hide.
Chorus:
For you I have given up the only real thing that I know.
For you there is no limit to how far I'd go.
I'd go anywhere and do anything for you, for you.

I always had this feeling I could not explain.
You were the only thing ever on my mind.
Nothing could ever stop this feeling.
It will be with me 'til the end of time.

Chorus

Bridge:
I would take all the stars out of the sky
Just to spend another moment by your side.
I would risk my life.
You know I would die,
For you.

Chorus

I felt good about including a more upbeat love song with some of my other slower, more romantic ballads (which were kind of my thing). Maybe Natasha was right. Maybe people were tired of listening to my slow, sappy love songs and wanted something a little more upbeat and inspiring. Even though the song is ultimately about unrequited love, it still had a faster tempo that I hoped the audience would enjoy.

As soon as I was done with sound check, Aiden took his turn.

"You sounded great," he told me. "I liked that new song you threw in there. What was the title of it?" "Thanks so much. It's called 'For You,'" I told him. "I'm really trying to step out of my comfort zone a bit more and try something new."

"Well, keep up the good work," he replied.

As Aiden stepped out on to the stage, he informed the sound guys that he was going to try out a new, unreleased song. *That's strange,* I thought. *He doesn't usually risk playing new stuff on tour, especially towards the end of the tour.*

As soon as I heard the first few notes, the song sounded familiar to me, even though it was unreleased.

"Looking back, it's hard to see,

What went wrong between you and me..."

I knew it was the song I had heard Aiden recording back in Austin. Was he trying to communicate something to me through the song? He told me that it wasn't about me, but was it really? I turned around and looked at Aiden as he was singing and noticed that he was staring straight at me while singing the song. Why did he have that power over me every time he looked at me? How did he make his eyes twinkle as he looked at you? As I found myself getting lost in the song, I shook my head and walked back to my dressing room.

No, I thought. *I will not get sucked in by him again. I can't. Why is he making me feel this way? Is he trying to string me along like this on purpose?*

Just a few moments later, I heard a knock at the door.

"Come in!" I shouted. It was the tour manager, Becky.

"Shelby? There is a call for you. It's your mom. It sounds urgent," she said.

"Okay. I'll come take it," I told her. "Is something wrong?"

"I don't know. You better talk to her and find out for yourself," she replied.

I got to the phone as quickly as I could. "Mom? What is it? What's wrong?" I asked.

"Shelby! You need to get home quick!" she said, urgently. "It's Dave! He's trying to take custody of the kids away from you!"

Chapter Twenty-Five

"What do you mean, Mom? How is he trying to take custody away?" I asked.

"He said you've been away and forcing them to stay at their grandmother's house and that you are a negligent mom. He had his lawyer draw up some papers," Mom said.

"What?! I can't believe this! He's allowed to ignore his kids for seven years, and I leave for a couple of weeks and this happens?" I said, nearly shouting. "Mom, do I need to come home right away?"

"It would be a good idea. He's already taken them to his house, and I don't even know what to do right now. Can he legally do that? Should I call the cops?" she asked.

"Mom, I'll try to get there as soon as I can. I have a show in a couple of hours, but I'll look right now for a flight out and be out of here soon," I said.

"I'm so sorry to do this to you, Honey. I know you were probably having the best time," she said.

"Actually, I think it's about time I come home anyway," I said. "I don't know what I was thinking, believing that I could be out on the road for this long away from my kids. Things are a little dramatic here right now, so this might be just the excuse I need."

I hung up the phone to see Aiden coming backstage after his soundcheck. I ran over and stopped him.

"Shelby? What's wrong?" he could tell just by looking at my face that something was up.

"Aiden, I have to go back home right away. I probably won't be able to get a flight until after the show, but I have to head back tonight. Dave is threatening to take the kids away from me," I told him. Tears began to well up in my eyes.

"What?! He can't do that, can he?" Aiden replied, shocked. "Shelby, I'm so sorry. This is all my fault. If you need someone to vouch for you or tell the courts how awesome of a mother you are, just let me know. I will be there as soon as you need me."

"Thank you for saying that Aiden. I don't know how much they would take your word for it since you've never really been around both me and the kids, but I appreciate the gesture," I told him, thankful that someone had my back.

I immediately got on my phone and started checking flight times. The earliest flight I could get was an hour after the show, so I would have to get out of there quickly. I raced back to my hotel room and packed as quickly as I could so I could rush out of the theater as soon as my set was over.

As soon as I got back to the theater, I had to change and get my hair and makeup done. I didn't have time to stop and think. I had to just play my setlist and get out of there as quickly as possible. I decided to scrap the new song and just play my rehearsed setlist from the other shows. It wasn't time to try something new. I had to just get it done and get out of there.

As I was exiting the stage, Aiden stopped me. "Why didn't you play that new song? I really liked it."

"I didn't want to try anything new tonight. I have enough going on as it is," I told him. "I'm so sorry I won't be there with you to perform in Athens. I hope you understand."

"That's no problem at all. Every now and then people have to perform without an opener. It's no big deal. You have bigger fish to fry," he said. "Are you going to stay for my set?"

"I don't think I can. My flight is leaving soon, so I need to get going to the airport," I told him. "I'm sorry. I wish I could stay and listen. I heard that song you played in Austin during your setlist. Are you going to play it tonight?"

"Maybe. I had a few other surprises up my sleeve, so it's a bummer you won't be here for it," he said, looking slightly crestfallen.

"I wish I could stay for it, but I really can't, Aiden. Good luck with the rest of the tour and with the new baby! I hope that you'll keep in touch," I told him. I could feel tears welling up in my eyes again, knowing that I was probably never going to see him again, and we weren't even able to have a proper goodbye. I felt like there were so many things that needed to be said, but I didn't even know where to begin, so I just left them unsaid.

"Goodbye, Aiden," I told him, holding back the tears.

"Goodbye, Shelby," he said.

"Aiden, they're ready for you," the stage manager told Aiden.

"Okay, coming," he answered.

I ran back to my dressing room as quickly as I could and gathered my things before calling for a taxi to the airport. Before I headed out, I decided to sneak a quick peek at Aiden's set to listen one more time before leaving.

"This is one you've never heard before," he told the crowd. "It's not even my song, but since I've heard it I haven't been able to get it out of my head. I hope you'll enjoy it as much as I do."

"Why are you doing this to me?
I was happy before you came into my life.
I had no reason to leave.
How can something so wrong feel so right?

I was with somebody else,
And you had tons of other girls pleading by your side.
I have battled with myself
But these feelings I just cannot hide.
Chorus:
For you I have given up the only real thing that I know.
For you there is no limit to how far I'd go.
I'd go anywhere and do anything for you, for you."

Chapter Twenty-Six

I didn't have time to stop and analyze what had just happened, although my mind held about a million whirling questions at that moment. I had to get to the airport and hop on that plane as quickly as I could. I was praying there would be no delays and that the flight would feel much faster than it was actually going to be. Why did Berlin have to be so far away from Texas? Never mind the inevitable jet lag, I was just eager to get back and get my kids.

As soon as I was checked in and waiting to board, I tried to give my mom a call, but I was still having issues with my cell phone making international calls. *Why does this have to be happening right now?* I thought to myself. *Why do I have to be going through a custody crisis, romantic crisis, and career crisis all at the same time?*

I tried to calm down my mind and think about anything else that may distract me from the monumental stress ball that was just hurled my way. I decided to take a walk around the terminal, hoping a little shopping, or perhaps picking up a book or magazine to read would calm my mind. As soon as I walked into the bookstore and started flipping through magazines, though, there was Aiden and Natasha. "Nashville Star and Wife Get Ready to Welcome New Baby!" The headline read.

Tears immediately began to well up in my eyes, and this time I couldn't hold them back. I just stood there by the newsstand bawling like a baby. The clerk of the store came up to me and said, "Sprichst du Englisch?"

"Yes, I do," I repiled.

"What is the matter?" the kind, old man asked.

"I'm sorry. I don't mean to be doing this in the middle of your store," I answered him.

"Did someone die?" he asked me.

"No, just sad about lost love," I informed him. He took the magazine from my hands.

"Ah, Aiden!" he recognized him immediately. "And baby! You know him?"

"Yes, I do," I said. "They are very lucky, aren't they?"

"Yes, Natasha very pretty," he answered.

"Yes. Yes, she is," I began to cry again.

"Oh no! You have baby, too, one day!" the man said, giving my shoulder a little squeeze.

"That's not…" I began, but then decided it was no use. "Yes, thanks." I turned back to him and smiled. I put the magazine back and instead grabbed a paperback that seemed to have absolutely nothing to do with my situation deciding it would be a better bet.

I went back to the gate, sat down, and tried to read the book, but it was no use. There was no way to get my mind off everything that had transpired in my life over the last few weeks. *How did it all come crashing down so horribly? Am I a bad person who did something to deserve this?*

I thought back to how this whole series of events had started. *What would have happened if I just decided not to talk to Aiden that day in Austin? What if I just smiled or waved at him and that was that? Would life be in better shape than it is right now, or would I have a whole mess of other circumstances I would be facing right now?*

Of course, there was no way of knowing what might have been. Just thinking the words "what might have been" to myself got me thinking about Aiden, once again. It was no use just sitting there dwelling on my own thoughts and feelings, so I decided to put it to paper in my own personal form of therapy and get the words out in the only way I knew how - through song.

"When she smiles you melt like butter.
You look in her eyes and she's the only one you see.
But what if there was another?
And what if that other girl was me?

When you come home at night she's the one you'll be kissing,
But what if there is something you have been missing?
What if you were with someone different?
What if she is not your heaven sent?

Chorus:
Why her, and not me?
Is there something about her I just can't see?
Why's she the one in your arms?
Boy, you know she'll only do you harm.
Why her, and not me?

I know that she is so pretty and petite.
I know you think that she is so great.
She really may not be what she seems.
Maybe someone else is meant for your fate.

She could turn out to be some evil heartbreaker.
Some other guy could come and try to take her.
What if she tried to treat you like you're in a prison?

You should think twice about your decision.

Chorus

Chapter Twenty-Seven

We landed at DFW Airport, and I immediately booked a ride to Dave's house to try to assess the situation. When I arrived at the door, he looked flabbergasted.

"Shelby?! What in the hell are you doing here?" he asked me.

"The more important question is, why are you trying to take my kids away from me?" I asked him furiously.

"I…I…" Dave didn't seem to know what to say. "I thought you were going to be gone at least for another week. I just thought the kids should take that time to spend it with their dad instead of being pawned off on their grandmother."

"Really? So, have you taken time off work, then? Have you been spending lots of quality time with them?" I asked him, crossing my arms.

"We've been spending lots of time together, haven't we, kids?" Dave turned around as the kids ran up to be to give me a huge hug.

"Mommy! We missed you so much!" Billy said. "We have been spending some time with Daddy, but mostly with the babysitter."

"I see," I turned back to Dave, glaring.

"That's not true, Billy. We've done lots of fun things together!" Dave said, trying to save face.

"Daddy mainly just sits on his phone or watches TV and tells us to play something together," said Bonnie.

"Bonnie, honey. What about that night we went out to eat together? That was fun, wasn't it?" he asked.

"Dad, getting fast foot last night was not all that fun," Billy replied.

"Bonnie, Billy, do you mind if your father and I have a little chat, just the two of us?" I asked the kids.

"Sure, Mommy, but you have to tell us all about your trip after that!" Bonnie said, excited to hear my stories.

"You got it," I told her.

As the kids ran into the other room to resume their board game, Dave and I had a seat on his couch.

"So, you want to explain what this is all about?" I asked him. "Did I do something to upset you? Do you think this is a fair deal on my part?"

Dave sighed. "No, you didn't do anything to upset me. I just thought this would be an opportunity to spend a little more time with my kids than I'm normally allowed. I feel like I'm missing out on so much of their lives." He looked genuinely sad.

"Then why wouldn't you take advantage of the time you have with them, instead of just ignoring them while they're here?" I asked him.

"I don't know," he replied. "I guess I don't really know how to spend time with them. I don't know what they're into or what they would enjoy doing with me."

"You know, they are capable of forming their own sentences. You could just ask them what they want to do or what they are into now," I told him.

"Yeah, I guess you're right," Dave said. "I feel like I am always the bad guy in the situation, and you are always the good guy, so I wanted to take the chance to try to be the good guy for once. I know

I wasn't there for all their concerts or games, so I thought if I could be there for them once while you weren't, I would be seen as the good guy for once."

I looked at him, questioningly. "You really think you are the bad guy in their eyes? Who do you think is the one who always has to give them consequences for their poor choices? Who do you think is the one making them clean their rooms or do their homework, when all they want to do is play video games? Are you the one who has to be the disciplinarian all the time?"

"No, I guess not," he said.

"They already see you as the fun one. You're the one who takes them out to eat, or takes them to the playground, or out for ice cream. I will admit, it would be nice if you put the phone away and didn't try to answer work calls or emails while you are with them, but they do think of you as the fun one who takes them to all the fun activities," I tried to reassure him.

"I guess you're right," Dave said. He sighed again. "Look, Shelby. I know I'm not the perfect dad and that I wasn't the perfect husband, but I'm really trying to get better. I'm going to try to leave work at work and focus more on the kids when they're with me. I'm asking you to meet me in the middle, though. Every other weekend with them is just not enough. Can we maybe agree to some more time, maybe every weekend, or after school on some days?"

I tried to assess if he was really being sincere or just trying to say the right thing at the right time. "I suppose we can have our lawyers look over the paperwork again and come up with a new agreement," I told him. "If you really keep good on your promises and actually spend time with them rather than ignoring them the whole time."

"Good. Then it's settled," Dave said. "So, tell me about these trips you've been taking. First to Los Angeles, and then to Europe? What happened while you were gone?"

I looked back at him and debated what exactly I should tell him. "Oh, you know," I said. "Just seeing what my life would be like if I actually put my songs out there rather than just keeping them to myself." I smiled.

Chapter Twenty-Eight

A few weeks passed, and things were somewhat back to my normal routine again. I was still on my leave from teaching, though, so I decided to focus some more on writing - not just songs, but also poems and possibly even a novel. I had some ideas in the works, and I wanted to go back to putting pen to paper for a while. It felt good getting all my ideas, feelings, musings, etc. out there instead of just keeping everything bottled up inside.

I also decided to sharpen my guitar-playing skills and take up piano as well. The musical bug had bitten me again, and I wanted to dive in full force.

One day, out of the blue, I received a knock at my door. I opened the door to find a courier with a package for me from Aiden. I opened it up to find a disc with the recordings we had done while in Los Angeles. It wasn't an officially licensed album or through a huge record company, but it was just a demo recording of the sessions Aiden and I had done together. Some were just of me singing, some were just Aiden singing, and some were a few of the songs we sang together. The CD was titled "What Might Have Been" and included the title song sung by Aiden.

I pulled it out of the case and slipped it into my CD player to give it a listen. As soon as Aiden's soulful voice came through the speakers, I began tearing up again, and eventually the floodgates just opened wide, and it all came pouring out. Just then, I noticed an extra verse thrown into "What Might Have Been" that I had never noticed before.

"Now I think back to the night.
When we gave it another try.
It all came flooding back,
And I wanted to freeze time.

If we could be us again,
I know we could get it right.
It's just you and me and no one else,
No need to apologize.

Chorus:
Then I won't have to ask myself every day,
What I could do differently this time to make you stay.
What could I have done way back then,
So, I don't constantly think about
What might have been."

I had to pause the song and stop to think. *Was that part always in the song, and I just never heard it? Did he add this part to the song after what happened in Paris?*

Here I was overanlyzing everything again. I didn't want to go down that road and think about everything that had happened in Europe, but I also knew that Aiden liked to hide his feelings in his song lyrics the same way I had always done. This time it didn't seem so hidden, though. It seemed to be clear as day that Aiden was trying to communicate something with me.

Chapter Twenty-Nine

I put that CD in a closet and forgot about it for a long time. I didn't want to focus on the past. There was nothing I could do about Aiden now. I had to just get over him and move on. I had done it once, so I knew I could do it again. All I needed to do is push the feelings down and forget about them. If I ever had a hard time with it, that's where my songwriting came in. Once I got those feelings down on paper, it was like a release. They might still be there, but at least I could pretend to just forget about them.

Life went on pretty normally for the next year. I decided to pitch some of my writing around to people and ended up getting a book deal with a local publisher. I still wasn't that comfortable performing my songs in front of people, so I put my songwriting on the back burner once again. At least I was still getting my creative juices going by writing some fiction. My first novel was due to the publisher in the spring. My editor asked for a meeting down in Austin to go over a few things.

It just so happened that the South by Southwest Music Festival was happening at the same time, so there was lots of music going on all around us. New and old artists alike were performing their songs at various venues around the city, some hoping to get discovered, others just looking to expand their audience and mingle with fellow musicians. The experience did make me long for those performing days again, but I just didn't have the courage anymore.

"Well, Shelby. We really like what you've submitted to us so far," Anne, my editor, informed me. "There are just a few tweaks we would like to make, including some more story line with the love interest and maybe some adjustments to his character."

"What sort of adjustments?" I asked.

"Well, he seems like too good of a guy," she said. "We need to add somewhat of a 'bad boy' quality. That's what readers are looking for in their love interests these days. They want to read about guys that are into S&M or seem like total jerks and end up being the loves of their lives. They can't just start out as nice guys and end up as nice guys."

"Why is that? Are you saying that doesn't exist in the real world?" I asked her.

"Honey, I know that doesn't exist in the real world," she said.

"Don't be so sure…" I told her.

"Do you know of some? If you do, please feel free to send them my way. I've been searching for years and have yet to find one single nice guy out there," she said, shrugging.

As if on cue, who but Aiden would walk through the door that very moment. *Of course, I would run into him in Austin again, of all places,* I thought. *What are the chances? And as soon as I mention nice guys? That's a little too on the nose.*

Aiden looked much different than I had last seen him. He had grown out his hair and grown a beard, but I would recognize that body and those sparkly blue eyes anywhere.

"What is it?" Anne asked. "You look like you just recognized someone. Is it someone famous?"

"Yes, it is," I said. "It's Aiden Walker. He just walked in the door."

"Oh my gosh! I love his music!" Anne said, enthusiastically.

"Yeah, he's pretty great," I said.

Aiden and I just looked at each other. He waved at me, smiled, and then kept walking. My heart sank. I swore to myself that if I ever ran into him again, I would just smile and wave, which is what I should have done the last time I saw him in Austin. He walked up to the counter to order a coffee, and I contemplated my next action. I just sat there, feeling unable to move.

"Shelby? Anyway, the love interest in this seems too good to be true. He is a tall, good-looking guy who does charity work on the side of his full-time job? Someone like that just does not exist in the real world," Anne informed me.

I glanced back over at Aiden. *He does seem too good to be true,* I thought. *And on top of everything else, someone else already has him.*

"Maybe you're right," I told Anne. "A guy like that would definitely not be single in this world. He would be snatched up right away by some amazing, gorgeous woman, and they would probably pop out a bunch of babies, leaving no chance for anyone else to snag him."

"That's a pretty specific scenario, but I'll take your word for it," Anne said. "So, I was thinking that we make him with dark hair, maybe a little mysterious, maybe give him a suit. Women love guys in suits these days…"

I saw Aiden start to head out the door, but before he did, he turned briefly in my direction. I thought for a moment that he was going to come over to our table, but he just looked at me, looked down, and headed out the door.

I didn't know what to do next. I felt stunned. I knew that Anne was talking to me, but I couldn't register what she was saying. I felt so numb, like I had let a piece of myself slip right through my fingers. I looked back up at Anne.

"Will you excuse me for just a moment?" I asked her.

I ran out the door as fast as I could to try to catch up to Aiden. I spotted him just a few yards ahead of me.

"Aiden!" I screamed at him.

He turned around and gave me a sad smile.

"Shelby," he said somberly. "How are you?"

"How am I?" I asked him. "Were you really just going to walk out of there without even saying a word to me?"

"I haven't heard from you in a while, so I figured you wanted nothing more to do with me. After I didn't hear from you for so long, I thought maybe you were mad at me, or just wanted to forget about me or something," he said.

"Trust me, I've been trying to forget about you for 20 years!" I shouted at him. "Do you know how impossible that is? Every song of yours I hear on the radio reminds me of you. Hell, even every love song I hear on the radio reminds me of you. Anytime I see someone who remotely looks like you or reminds me of you in some slight, little way, I think about you. Anytime I sit down to write a song, I think about you. Anytime I even look at my guitar, I think about you. Forgetting about you is not an option at this point!"

I knew I was making a scene and getting myself worked up, but I couldn't help myself. I had pushed my feelings down for so long that I had all these pent-up emotions just waiting to pour out of me.

"Geez, Shelby," Aiden said. "I had no idea!" He looked from the ground, and then back into my eyes. "You know, I never stopped thinking about you either. I've written so many songs lately that just pour out of me, and every single one seems to be about you."

"What about Natasha?" I asked him.

"Natasha and I split up in the winter," he told me with a sad look on his face. "The baby wasn't mine. Once we got home from the tour, I went to the doctor with her and learned about the timeline of conception, and it couldn't have possibly been mine because I was away. She cried and confessed to the entire thing."

"Oh, Aiden. I'm so sorry," I told him, stroking his arm.

"That's okay. Of course, I am extremely bummed about it, but we probably weren't the best fit anyway. She was starting to get a little clingy and needy. She didn't seem to fully grasp what it meant to be a touring musician. She expected me to be at her beck and call all the time."

"So, what are you doing now, then?" I asked him.

"Well, I'm checking out South by Southwest this weekend, trying to maybe scout some new talent for collaborations. I might perform at a couple of small shows discreetly. I haven't really decided yet. It will be a last-minute surprise visit if I do," he answered.

"How long are you going to be in town?" I asked him.

"Probably the next couple of days. How long are you in town?" he asked.

"Well, I was going to leave this afternoon," I said. I thought about the possibility of spending more time with Aiden. Did I really want to put myself through that again? Would we get back to where we left off? Now that we were both single at the same time, would we even still feel the same way about each other, or had the magic worn off?

"You are more than welcome to hang out with me for the rest of the weekend," Aiden said. "Unless you need to get back right away."

I thought about what I had to go back to. I didn't have the kids that weekend. All I had going on was my meeting with the editor and then my empty weekend and empty house to go home to. Somehow, I thought that staying there with Aiden would feel more like home to me.

I looked at Aiden. "You know what? I would love to stay and hang out with you for the rest of the weekend. I don't want to look back on today and wonder what might have been."

Printed in the USA
CPSIA information can be obtained
at www.ICGtesting.com
CBHW032113130924
14158CB00053B/1064

9 781957 262307